THE BIKE TYCOON
A Tandem Original

'When you say "partner," ' Fonzie asked, 'does that mean we're going in business together or we're going out west some place and play cowboy?'

'It must be business,' Marion told him. 'Out west, I think it's "podner!" '

'Business it is,' Howard said. 'Fonzie, I am willing to set you up in your own operation – for a cut of the profits, of course.'

'Howard,' Marion said dubiously, 'are you sure you want to—'

'This is too big an opportunity to pass up!' he said. 'The profit margin is unbelievable.' He faced Fonzie again. 'We'll rent a store,' he said. 'You can rebuild the bikes in the back and we'll have display space in the front. And, one store, that's only the beginning. As soon as the first store is in the black – which shouldn't take more than a week – we'll start opening branches. We'll need a training program, of course – you'll have to teach other mechanics how to rebuild bikes, so they can take over the branch stores. Then, we'll start expanding throughout the state. Within two or three years, we'll have a whole chain of stores all across the country!'

Fonzie looked somewhat dazed. 'How did that happen? When I sat down to eat, all I had was a job at a garage. I haven't even got to dessert yet and already I'm a tycoon.'

Also in *Tandem*

THE BIKE TYCOON

HAPPY DAYS! 2
THE BIKE TYCOON

William Johnston

A TANDEM BOOK
published by
TANDEM PUBLISHING Ltd

A Tandem Book
Published in 1977
by Tandem Publishing Ltd.
A Howard and Wyndham Company
44 Hill Street, London W1X 8LB

Copyright © 1976 by Paramount Pictures Corporation

Printed in Great Britain by
Hazell Watson & Viney Ltd, Aylesbury, Bucks.

ISBN 0 426 18382 7

ONE

At the garage where he was employed, Fonzie was
working painstakingly on the engine of a racy looking Harley Davidson motorcycle. He was being
watched by Richie Cunningham, who was sitting
crosslegged on a fender of a customer's car.

"That's a doozy," Richie commented.

"No, that's a sparkplug, Cunningham," Fonzie responded. "If you're gonna talk motors, know what
you're talking about."

"I meant the bike," Richie said. "That's about the
sharpest looking machine I've ever seen in here. And
you get the best bikes in town to work on."

"That's because when a guy owns a bike like this,
he don't want no nerd tinkering with it," Fonzie said.
"In the world of mechanics, Cunningham, The Fonz
is like a fine surgeon. Look around," he said. "You
don't see no hammer around here, do you? The Fonz
would no more use a hammer on a bike motor than a
surgeon would go after some guy's appendix with a
hatchet."

"You're good, all right," Richie agreed.

"Good? The Fonz is spectacular. I ought to have an

1

audience when I work on a bike. You know how, when a surgeon is operating on a human body, other doctors sit around in a balcony and watch his technique? What this garage needs is a balcony."

"So other mechanics could watch you, you mean."

"Not just mechanics. Doctors, too," Fonzie said. "It wouldn't hurt no doctor to watch The Fonz do a tune-up. When I adjust the gap on a sparkplug, you get the kind of arc that no artist could paint—including that guy that cut off his ear while he was painting the ceiling while on his back."

"Those are two different painters, Fonz," Richie said. "Van Gogh cut off his ear and Michelangelo painted the ceiling."

"Whichever," Fonzie replied. "Those doctors could still learn something from The Fonz. They wouldn't give a guy a check-up one day on his whatsit and have him kick the bucket the next day with whatchamacallit stones in his thingamajig."

"Fonz, if you're going to talk anatomy, know what you're talking about."

"I still say—" Fonzie interrupted himself, looking toward the garage doorway. A young man in jodhpurs and riding boots and carrying a riding crop had appeared. "If you're looking for your horse, it didn't go through here," Fonzie told him.

"My horse died," the young man replied sadly, entering the garage.

"Then you might as well change your clothes," Fonzie said. "I haven't never heard of no horse coming back." Then a sudden realization struck him. "Are you looking for a *new* horse? You're in the wrong place. This is a car garage, not a barn. Anytime we get a horse in here, we take out the power—for a spare part—and throw the rest away."

Richie laughed. "That's pretty good, Fonz—horse power."

"Cunningham, don't explain my jokes to me."

"It isn't a horse I'm looking for," the young man said, stopping near the front wheel of the bike that Fonzie was working on. "I couldn't ever own another horse . . . not after Charlotte Bronte . . ."

"Heyyyyy—what happened?" Fonzie asked sympathetically. "Some dame knock off your nag? I had a thing like that happen to me once. Her name was Harriet. She had wedding bells on her mind. She was a ding-a-ling. When I told her I wasn't the marrying kind, she let the air out of my tires. That wasn't as bad as your case, of course. When some dame knocks off your nag, you can't pump it up again."

"No, Charlotte Bronte was the name of my horse," the young man said. He sighed tragically. "There can never be another Charlotte. So, I've decided to become a cyclist."

"You're looking for a bike?"

"Precisely." With his riding crop he tapped the motorcycle that Fonzie was working on. "What's her bloodline?" he asked.

"He's a he," Fonzie replied. "He's out of Harley by Davidson.

Crouching, the young man sighted across the handlebars. "Nice withers," he said. "What's his name?" he asked, straightening.

"Yeah," Fonzie replied.

"Pardon?"

"That's his name—What's-his-name," Fonzie told him.

"Would you sell?" the young man asked.

"Who knows?" Fonzie replied, becoming cagey. "When you raise a bike from a colt, it's not easy to let go."

"I understand," the young man said. "Losing Charlotte Bronte was like losing a part of me—my heart."

"With me, I guess it would be more like the fuel pump," Fonzie said.

"Fonz," Richie began, "you can't—"

"Butt out, Cunningham. You're too young to know what it's like to be a mother."

"But, Fonz, that bike—"

Ignoring Richie's protest, Fonzie addressed the young man again. "However," he said, "you look like the kind of guy that would give this bike the same kind of care I would give it myself. No spurs—right?"

"Oh, never!" the young man replied.

"And premium oats in the gas— I mean, premium gas in the oats— What I'm saying is, you wouldn't never foul up the plugs with no cheap gas."

"Fonz," Richie said, persisting, "you can't sell what doesn't be—"

Fonzie continued to ignore him. "You can have the bike for three-hundred clams," he told the young man.

The young man looked mildly distressed. "May I make a counter offer?" he said. "Why don't I pay you in money and you can buy your own clams?"

"Clams *is* money," Fonzie informed him. "You got to learn that if you're gonna ride a bike. Clams is motorcycle talk for cash."

"I see," the young man said, brightening. "And how much is three-hundred clams?"

"That's three-hundred simoleons," Fonzie told him.

The expression of distress returned to the young man's face.

"Dollars."

"Done and done!" the young man said, beaming. He reached into his jacket. "I'll write you a check!"

"Fonz, can I say something now?" Richie asked.

"At a sacred moment like this, while I'm making three-hundred clams?" Fonzie objected. "Where's your decency, Cunningham? Why don't you just go out and tip over gravestones?"

"Here you are," the young man said, handing Fonzie a check. "Three-hundred linoleums."

"That's simoleons."

"Whatever," the young man said. He stepped back and looked admiringly at the bike. Then suddenly he frowned. "That saddle has no stirrups," he said. "How do I mount?"

"You got a little learning to do," Fonzie advised him. "First off, you got to start using your eyes. Now, if you look close, you will see that this bike is not as high as a horse—right?"

"By, George, that *is* right!"

"So, to get on, you just throw a leg over," Fonzie told him.

Following Fonzie's instruction, the young man got aboard the motorcycle.

"You got the right idea, but you got the wrong leg," Fonzie said. "You're sitting on it backwards."

"Sorry," the young man said, reversing his position.

Fonzie then taught him how to start the engine, how to shift the gears, and how to use the brakes. "That's all there is to it," he said, when he finished. "Except that it's got a motor and a transmission and no tail, it's just like a horse."

The young man revved the engine—vroooom-vroom-vroom! The motor backfired.

"And it snorts like a horse," Fonzie said.

"Am I free to go now?" the young man asked.

"Giddyap," Fonzie replied.

"Tally-ho!" the young man cried out, accelerating. And the bike roared across the garage and out the doorway. The sound of the engine quickly faded.

"That's the way it goes," Fonzie said blithely, "another day, another three-hundred simoleons."

"But, Fonz—"

"Cunningham, what is biting you?" Fonzie asked. "I'm trying to make my daily three-hundred bucks, and you stand around sounding like a motorboat, but, but, but, but, but, but!"

"Fonz, don't you realize what you just did? A customer brought that bike in to have it repaired and you *sold* it. You sold something that didn't belong to you! What are you going to tell the customer?"

"Is that what you're but, but, butting about? Cool it, Cunningham. That wasn't no customer's bike. That was my bike."

Richie groaned. "Fonz, don't give me that. I know your bike when I see it. Your bike is parked outside the garage—I saw it when I came in."

"You never heard of a guy having *two* bikes?"

"Two bikes?"

"Yeah. I picked up that other bike a couple weeks ago," Fonzie told him. "The guy that had it plowed into a tree with it. It was a wreck. But, I figured maybe I could use some of the parts. So, I offered him twenty bucks for it and he said okay."

"But—"

"Cunningham, if you're gonna keep but, but, butting, get out of here and go down to the lake and rent yourself out to some fisherman, will you?"

"That bike you sold was not a wreck," Richie said. "It was a beauty."

"Yeah, I know. When I got the parts back here to the garage, they became a kind of a challenge. They kept saying, 'Put me back together.' They wouldn't let up. I'd be in the john and I'd hear them calling through the door to me, 'Put me back together.' I'd lock up at night and start to leave and I'd hear them crying out to me in the dark, 'Put me back together.' It was a heart-rending plea, Cunningham."

"Did you put them back together?"

Fonzie peered at him. "What do you think I'm telling you this story for? You think I'm going for an Academy Award or something? Yeah, I put them back together. That was them that that guy just rode out of here on, chasing some fox."

"Fonz, that's fantastic!" Richie said.

"What do you expect? Anything The Fonz does has got a little of the fantastic in it."

"I mean, you bought that wreck for twenty dollars and you just sold it for *three-hundred* dollars!"

Fonzie shrugged. "Some days are like that," he said. "If I live to be as old as Methuselah, I might even have another day like that someday."

That evening, at dinner, Richie told the other members of the Cunningham family—his father, Howard, his mother, Marion, and his sister, Joanie—about Fonzie's feat, rebuilding a wrecked motorcycle and selling it at a profit.

"Yeah," Fonzie said, when he had been congratulated, "you know what I been thinking I might do? I might go into the business."

"What business, Arthur?" Marion asked.

"The business Richie just told you about. A lot of guys wreck their bikes. What's to stop me from buying up the wrecks and putting them back together and selling them?"

Marion frowned. "I don't know," she replied.

"You don't know what?"

"I don't know what's to stop you," she replied. "Wasn't that your question?"

"Nothing is to stop me," Fonzie said.

"Well, if I were you," Howard said, "I'd think about it again ... and then again and again. There are a lot of pitfalls lying in wait for the small businessman, Fonzie."

"Hey! I'm not *that* small," Fonzie said. "I'm as big as you are, and you do okay in business."

"When I say 'small businessman,'" Howard explained, "I'm talking about my hardware store in comparison, say, to General Motors. GM is big business and I'm small business."

"How tall *is* the General, Howard?" Marion asked.

"Just tall enough that his head reaches his hat, Marion."

"Dad, I don't see what problems Fonzie would have, though," Richie said. "It's so simple. All he has to do is buy wrecks, fix them up, then sell them."

"But would it really be worth his time?" Howard replied. "I'm sure there's a lot of work involved in rebuilding a motorcycle. And how much profit could there be in it?"

"Well, he bought the wreck for twenty bucks and sold it for three-hundred dollars," Richie said.

Howard stared at him. *"Three-hundred dollars?"*

Richie nodded.

"But it wasn't all profit," Fonzie said.

"Oh . . ."

"Yeah, one night I worked so late on rebuilding the bike, I had to get two dinners from Arnold's," Fonzie explained. "So, from that three-hundred clams, you got to subtract two hamburgers and a chocolate shake."

"Three-hundred dollars!" Howard said again, awed by the profit. "Do you realize that that is a return of fifteen dollars on every dollar invested!"

"Not according to my arithmetic," Marion said. "I get fourteen dollars and one-twentieth of two hamburgers and a shake."

"Even so, that's a phenomenal profit," Howard said. "Fonzie, I think you're right—you *should* go into the business."

"Yeah, my thought exactly," Fonzie said. "The next time I come across a wrecked bike, I'm gonna do the same thing again."

"No, that isn't a business, that's a hobby," Howard said. "For it to be a business, you have to devote your full time to it."

"I got too much to do at the garage to do that."

"Fonzie, that job at the garage is peanuts compared to this," Howard told him. "Compare your salary to what you made by selling that *one* rebuilt bike."

Fonzie grimaced. "When I'm doing the figuring, do I have to count in the hamburgers and shake?"

"Impossible," Joanie said. "Peanuts cannot be divided by hamburgers and shakes."

"Hold it!" Fonzie said. "This is starting to sound like one of those problems I used to get in school. If

Jack and Jill went up the hill with a bucket of water and Jack fell down, how many oranges are there in a bushel-and-a-half of grapefruit? If that is what business is, count me out."

"Don't worry about the arithmetic, partner," Howard said. "I'll handle that end of it."

The others peered at him questioningly.

"When you say 'partner,'" Fonzie asked, "does that mean we're going in business together or we're going out west someplace and play cowboy?"

"It must be business," Marion told him. "Out west, I think it's 'podner.'"

"Business it is," Howard said. "Fonzie, I am willing to set you up in your own operation—for a cut of the profits, of course."

"Howard," Marion said dubiously, "are you sure you want to—"

"This is too big an opportunity to pass up!" he said. "The profit margin is unbelievable." He faced Fonzie again. "We'll rent a store," he said. "You can rebuild the bikes in the back and we'll have display space in the front. And, one store, that's only the beginning. As soon as the first store is in the black—which shouldn't take more than a week—we'll start opening branches. We'll need a training program, of course—you'll have to teach other mechanics how to rebuild bikes, so they can take over the branch stores. Then, we'll start expanding throughout the state. Within two or three years, we'll have a whole chain of stores all across the country!"

Fonzie looked somewhat dazed. "How did that happen? When I sat down to eat, all I had was a job at a garage. I haven't even got to dessert yet and already I'm a tycoon."

"It's the American success story, Fonz," Richie said.

"Yes, Arthur," Marion said. "I'm sure General Motors wasn't always a general. He must have started as a private."

"What do you say, partner?" Howard asked.

"I don't know ... it's not The Fonz," Fonzie said. "I can't picture no tycoon in a leather jacket."

"Howard Hughes was a tycoon, wasn't he?" Joanie said. "I read in Hedda Hopper that he wore tennis shoes."

"If I got to do that, it's no deal," Fonzie said. "How am I gonna get tennis shoes on inside my boots?"

"No, Fonzie, what Joanie means is that when you're a tycoon you can wear anything you want to," Richie explained.

"That's what I do now," Fonzie said. "Okay," he said to Howard, "if I don't have to change, it's a deal."

Howard beamed. "We'll be tycoons together!" He turned to Marion. "Incidentally, have you seen my tennis shoes around lately?"

Answering a knock at the door that evening, Richie found Potsie and Ralph there.

"Want to go to a movie?" Potsie asked.

"It's a great one—*The Giant Cow That Licked Up Salt Lake City*," Ralph said.

"I don't think I want to go," Richie replied. "I'm listening to my father explain business to Fonzie." He then told them about the plan to open a used motorcycle shop.

"Let's stay," Potsie said to Ralph. "The giant cow will still be playing tomorrow night."

"That's not play when you lick up a whole city," Ralph said.

They headed for the living room, where Howard and Fonzie were talking. When they reached there, Howard was discussing business taxes.

"Hey, wait a minute," Fonzie said. "Who gets these taxes?"

"The government," Howard replied.

"Yeah, Fonz, that's where the government gets its money," Potsie said.

"If the government wants money, why can't it get a job like everybody else?" Fonzie replied.

"The government does have a job," Howard told him. "Its job is to collect the taxes."

"Why don't we just cut out the taxes?" Fonzie asked. "Then we won't need no government to collect them."

"Well, actually, the government does other things besides collecting taxes," Howard explained. "The government runs the Army and the Navy and—"

"Who needs it?" Fonzie said. "Listen, just last week, I was riding up Main Street and this army convoy comes by. All these trucks. Traffic was stopped. I was stuck there for almost an hour while this convoy goes by. You mean to tell me I got to *pay* for that?"

"Fonz, the Army protects the country," Richie said.

"The Fonz don't need no protecting. Anybody that needs it, let them pay the taxes. What I make, it goes into my pocket."

"Well . . . we'll discuss taxes again some other time," Howard said. "Now, advertising . . . It's important to decide how much advertising we're going to do so that we can have an advertising budget. You see, the price of our product is determined, in part, by how much it costs us to produce and sell that product. And, advertising, of course, is part of the selling cost."

Fonzie stared at him blankly.

"Let's say it costs us twenty dollars to buy a wrecked bike," Howard said. "And, let's say that we spend another one hundred dollars, per bike, for parts and labor and rent and advertising and so on and so on. So far, that's an outlay of one hundred and twenty dollars. Obviously, then, in order to make a profit, we've got to sell the rebuilt bike for *more* than one hundred and twenty dollars."

"You got to go through all that rigamarole to figure that out?" Fonzie said. "No wonder you business guys get heartburn. With my way, it's so easy. A guy comes into the garage, he says, 'How much you want for that?' and I say 'Three-hundred clams.' "

"Yes, but how did you arrive at that figure?" Howard asked.

"It was the first number that popped in my head."

Howard shook his head. "That's no way to do business, Fonzie."

"At your store," Fonzie said, "how many times have you bought something for twenty bucks and sold it for three-hundred?"

"Never. I couldn't—"

"I rest my case," Fonzie said, breaking in. "Anyway, what do we need advertising for? I didn't need no advertising to sell that bike to that guy that lost his horse."

"But that was a fluke," Howard said.

"No, a fluke is a fish," Fonzie said. "This guy didn't lose no fish, he lost his horse. Who ever heard of a fish named Charlotte Bronte?"

"I mean it was pure chance that he came into the garage at a time when you had a rebuilt bike for sale," Howard said. "You can't depend on chance to get customers. You have to let them know where you are and what you have for sale."

"I'll stick up a sign at Arnold's," Fonzie said. "That won't cost nothing."

"Well . . . we'll discuss pricing and advertising some other time . . ." Howard said. "Now, customer relations—"

"Let's talk about that some other time, too, when we're talking about all that other stuff," Fonzie said, rising. "I'm getting heartburn from all this gab. I think I got to go down to Arnold's and put out the fire with a wet malt."

"Actually, I'm going to be handling the business end of the operation," Howard said, "so I suppose it isn't absolutely necessary for you to understand all the details."

"Want to see *The Giant Cow That Licked Up Salt Lake City*?" Ralph asked Fonzie.

"No, I'm waiting for the sequel: *The Giant Cow That Got So Thirsty When It Licked Up Salt Lake City, It Had To Go Over And Drink Up Lake Erie*," Fonzie replied, departing.

On the way to Arnold's, Fonzie rode his bike, slowly, and Richie, Potsie, and Ralph walked alongside.

"Did you notice something about your old man?" Fonzie said to Richie. "By the time we left, he wasn't talking about becoming a tycoon any more."

"I think he's having some second thoughts," Richie

replied. "It's probably not very easy being your business partner, Fonz."

"From now on, it'll be easier on him," Fonzie said. "I'm not going to listen to anything he tells me any more. That way, he won't have to try to explain it."

"You're all heart, Fonz," Potsie said.

"What are you going to call your store?" Ralph asked Fonzie.

"I'm gonna call it a store. What do you think I'm going to call it, a chimpanzee?"

"I mean what are you going to name it?"

"I haven't thought of anything yet."

"Where is it going to be?" Potsie asked. "It'll have to be a big place, with space for rebuilding the bikes and even more space for showing them off to customers. Need somebody to do the selling, Fonz? I could do that."

"Me, too," Ralph said. "I'm a natural-born salesman. I've got personality."

Fonzie offered no comment.

"Hey, Fonz, I said I had personality," Ralph said. "Aren't you going to insult me?"

Fonzie still remained silent.

"Fonz . . ." Richie said.

At last, Fonzie spoke. "I just discovered a fly in the ointment," he said. "All that space we're gonna need for rebuilding bikes and putting them out so customers can see them—we're not gonna need it."

"Fonz, you're not backing out are you?" Richie asked.

"I'm not backing out. There's nothing to back out from. Ask yourself this question: where are we gonna get all these bikes that we're gonna rebuild? Is Santa

Claus coming and dropping them down the chimney?"

"Wrecked bikes, Fonz."

"Yeah, wrecked bikes. But, the way our old man is talking—like a tycoon—we're gonna be peddling maybe a hundred bikes a week, what with all our branch stores. So, I repeat the question: where are we gonna get all these wrecked bikes?"

"A lot of bikes get wrecked, Fonz," Ralph said.

"Not at that rate. At that rate, bike-wrecking would have to become a patriotic civic project. Volunteers would have to buy bikes brand-new and take them out and wreck them on purpose."

"Well . . . maybe there will be an epidemic of bike wrecks or something . . ." Richie said.

"What is more likely is, we'll go into and out of business the same day," Fonzie said.

They reached Arnold's Drive-In and Fonzie parked next to another motorcycle.

"Hey, that's a class machine," he said, indicating the other bike.

"It's Harold Wilburmeyer's," Ralph said.

"That rich kid?"

Ralph nodded. "It's the second new bike he's had this month," he said. "After a couple weeks, he says, they're unsanitary—from the tires touching the road. What he needs is somebody to run along in front of him with a broom and clean the streets."

"Stay here," Fonzie said to Richie, Ralph, and Potsie, heading toward the entrance to the drive-in.

"Fonz—where are you going?"

"I'm gonna start the business rolling," he replied, disappearing into Arnold's.

"Maybe he's going to buy Harold's bike and wreck it," Potsie said.

"I don't think there would be much profit in that," Richie replied.

"Maybe he's going to wreck Harold and inherit his bike," Ralph suggested.

Richie shook his head. "That wouldn't be cool," he said. "The Fonz wouldn't do anything uncool."

A few moments later, Fonzie returned. He was accompanied by Harold Wilburmeyer, a chubby boy, whose natural expression was an insipid sneer.

"I have been challenged to a race around the parking lot," Fonzie announced.

"How did that happen?" Potsie asked suspiciously.

"Who knows? I was standing there making polite chit-chat with Harold here and all of a sudden it came up in the conversation, a total surprise. You could have knocked me over with a feather bed."

"The Wilburmeyers are all daredevils," Harold explained.

"You guys," Fonzie said to Richie, Potsie, and Ralph, "get the back seats out of these cars parked here and fling them around for padding. I'm not no daredevil like Harold here. I don't want to get hurt if the race gets too fast for me and I get flung off my bike."

Harold chuckled evilly, relishing the idea.

"What this is gonna be is a race in a circle," Fonzie said to Harold, as Richie, Potsie, and Ralph began collecting seats from the parked cars. "You know what a circle is?"

"One of those round things?"

"You got it. We go round and round the cars. Round and round and round," he went on, making revolving motions, "and round and round and round—"

Harold, following the revolving motion with his eyes, began to look a bit dizzy.

"—and round and round and round—"

"All set, Fonz," Richie called out.

Fonzie and Harold Wilburmeyer got on their bikes and started the motors.

"How long are we going to race?" Harold asked.

"I'll let you know when it's over," Fonzie told him. "Are you ready?"

"Oh, boy!" Harold said. "I'm going to beat The Fonz! With this new bike, I can't lose!"

"Yeah . . . just answer the question: are you ready?"

"Ready!"

"Go!" Fonzie said.

Harold's bike roared off, taking the lead. Fonzie followed, riding casually, keeping pace with Harold, but remaining several yards behind him. Round and round the bikes went, in circle after circle after circle.

"Fonz isn't even trying," Potsie said puzzled.

"But I think Harold is trying a little too hard," Richie said. "Something's wrong with him . . . he's beginning to look a little strange."

"He was never any beauty," Ralph said.

"There's something about his eyes . . ." Potsie said. "Is he getting dizzy?"

"How could he help it?" Richie said. "He's been going around and around in circles like that for— Oh-oh!"

Harold's bike was beginning to sway from side to side.

"How come Fonzie isn't getting dizzy?" Potsie wondered.

At that moment, a mishap occurred. Harold's bike turned, but Harold didn't. Leaving the motorcycle, he went diving into a pile of car seats. The bike, without a helmsman, roared out of the parking lot and crashed into a telephone pole, then fell apart, a wreck.

Harold Wilburmeyer was rising as Fonzie and the others reached the pile of car cushions. Staggering, he looked about dazedly.

"You okay?" Fonzie asked.

"I will be as soon as the world stops turning," Harold replied. "What happened?"

"I think maybe you got a little dizzy from going around and around and around—"

Harold clapped his hands to his ears. "Don't say that! I'm getting dizzy again!"

"Heyyyyy!" Fonzie said, looking toward the street. "Too bad about your bike. That is a total mess!"

"Oh, that's all right," Harold said. "Dad will get me a new one. What bothers me is, I had a chance to beat The Fonz and I muffed it!"

Fonzie smiled. "When you get your new bike, maybe I'll let you try again," he said.

"Would you?" Harold said rapturously.

"It depends on if I need another wrecked— I mean, it just depends," Fonzie replied. "But, since you brought up the subject of the wrecked bike, you want to sell that one you just turned into spare parts? I'll give you twenty bucks for it."

"Sure, why not?" Harold replied. "It was becoming unsanitary anyway."

Fonzie handed him a twenty-dollar bill. "Now, you better go in and sit down and get over your dizzies," Fonzie said. "Have a Bromo or something. It's on me."

"Thanks!"

"Take it out of the twenty," Fonzie said, shooing him toward the drive-in.

"Now, we're in business—we got a wreck," Fonzie said, when Harold had gone.

"Just one thing, Fonz," Richie said. "How come when you and Harold were going around and around in circles, Harold got dizzy but you didn't?"

"Simple," Fonzie replied. "I know how dangerous that can be, going around and around like that. So, I kept my eyes closed."

TWO

Standing on a ladder, Richie was painting the name across the front of the store that Fonzie and Howard had rented for their used bike business. So far, he had painted:

FONZIE'S BIKET

Fonzie, standing on the sidewalk below, was overseeing the project.

"Hey!" Fonzie called up. "That sign goes downhill!"

"Fonz, it couldn't," Richie replied. "I drew those straight lines across before I started, and I'm keeping the letters inside the lines."

"Yeah, only when you drew those straight lines across, you drew them downhill," Fonzie told him. "Or, if you started at the other side, you drew them *up*hill."

"Oh . . . Do you want me to clean off what I've done and start again?"

"Nah, I kind of like it going downhill," Fonzie replied. "It's racy, speedy. When you look at it, it puts you in mind of a bike charging down a hill, all out."

At that moment, Potsie and Ralph arrived.

"That's a great name—Fonzie's Biket!" Ralph said. "What does it mean?"

"The sign is not finished yet, Tweedle dumb-dumb," Fonzie told him. "It's gonna be Fonzie's Biketeria. You know—like in cafeteria."

"Are you going to serve food with the bikes, Fonz?" Potsie asked.

"Only to you, Snow White," Fonzie replied. "You get a poison apple. No, I'm not gonna serve food. What Biketeria means is, it's a cafeteria-like operation. You walk in, you buy what you want, and you get out. No standing around. I got work to do, re-building those bikes, I don't want a lot of nerds taking up my time with chit-chat."

"I understand, all business," Potsie said. He looked through the doorway into the store. "I thought it would be bigger," he said.

"It's the perfect size," Fonzie told him. "Come on in and I'll show you."

They entered the store. The front section was vacant. At the rear there were two wrecked motorcycles, a collection of spare parts and Fonzie's tools.

"You see?" Fonzie said. "Up here, you got the front end and, back there, you got the back end. What more could you want? A middle? If you had a middle, you'd have to climb over it to get to the front or back."

Potsie and Ralph were watching a column of ants that was on the march toward the front door.

"They finally gave up and they're moving out," Fonzie said, pleased.

Potsie and Ralph looked at him perplexedly.

"This used to be a bakery," Fonzie explained. "This was home to those ants. They got very confused when the bakery moved out and we moved in with those wrecked bikes. They tried to eat a fender. They thought the shiny paint was icing."

Richie joined them, having finished painting the sign. "All done," he said.

"Oh, say, Rich, there was something I was going to mention," Potsie said. "That sign runs uphill."

"Downhill," Fonzie said.

Potsie shook his head. "It looks uphill to me," he said. "It makes me think of a bike, out of gas, trying to make it to the top of a hill, sputtering. I don't think that's very good for business."

"Downhill. And the bike is charging, going all out," Fonzie insisted.

"Okay. If you say so. But—"

A middle-aged woman, looking harried, had entered the store. "Two loaves of bread," she said to Fonzie, opening her purse, "and how are your bagels today?"

"Not so good," Fonzie replied. "But the used bikes are fresh."

"All right—a dozen," the woman said. "And I want to order an angel food cake for next Tuesday—it's my daughter's birthday. White icing, and in pink lettering, I want—" Interrupting herself, she peered puzzledly at Fonzie. "Your used bikes are fresh?"

"This is not no bakery any more, lady," Fonzie told her. He pointed. "Look—there goes the ants."

"Oh, my! I wonder where the bakery is."

"Follow the ants," Fonzie suggested.

"I don't think there's time for that," the woman said, departing. "It will be next Tuesday before those ants ever get to the sidewalk."

"Well, we just had our first customer," Fonzie said,

pleased. "Maybe I should have sold her a tire and told her it was a giant bagel."

Howard arrived. "Who was that woman?" he asked.

"She thought this was still a bakery, Dad."

"Didn't she see the sign?"

"Maybe she don't read downhill," Fonzie said.

"Have we had any *other* customers?" Howard asked.

"Dad, this is the first day," Richie said. "Nobody even knows that the store is open."

"Besides , what would we sell?" Fonzie said. "I haven't got those bikes rebuilt yet."

"Then why are you just *standing* here!" Howard said.

"Hey, take it easy," Fonzie said. "Rome wasn't rebuilt in a day, you know. That goes for bikes, too."

"I know, I know," Howard responded, calming himself. "I'm just concerned about my investment. There's the rent for the store and the paint for the sign and the cost of those replacement parts ... I'd like to see some money coming in, instead of all going out."

"Okay, I'll get started," Fonzie said, moving on toward the rear of the soare.

"We've got to start advertising," Howard said, as he and Richie and Potsie and Ralph trailed after Fonzie. "I think I'll put an ad in tomorrow's paper."

"No ads in no papers," Fonzie said.

"Why not?" Howard asked. "I advertise the hardware store in the papers. I get a lot of business that way."

"Yeah, but you got a different type of customer at the hardware store," Fonzie said. "They're probably all high school graduates."

"I don't get the connection."

"I know bikers," Fonzie told him. "Putting an ad in a newspaper for bikers to read would be like stuffing your money down a manhole."

"Rat hole," Richie said.

"Whatever. The bikers I know don't read. And the ones that do read, don't read newspapers. What they read is comic books—the kind that if you get caught in school with them, you get sent down to the principal's office."

"Do they watch TV, then?" Howard asked.

Fonzie nodded. "Very high on 'The Mickey Mouse Club.'"

"We'll have to advertise on television, then," Howard decided. "That makes sense. That's where our competition advertises."

"Who's our competition?" Richie asked.

"Friendly Foster—right?" Fonzie said, addressing Howard. "He's got the only other used bike shop in town. I've seen his ads on TV. He's got good ads. But he's got lousy bikes."

"Well, we're going to have both," Howard said.

"*Lousy* ads and lousy bikes?"

"Good ads and *good* bikes," Howard said. "I have a great idea for a TV ad. Plain and simple—and, above all, sincere. We're going to have you, Fonzie, standing in front of the camera and describing the merchandise."

"You're not the first one to have that great idea," Fonzie said. "That's what Friendly Foster does."

"But we have you," Howard pointed out. "The viewers will believe you. You're The Fonz."

"I can't argue with you on that."

"We'll need an advertising agency to handle this,"

Howard said. He headed for the door. "I'll get right on it!"

"Don't step on the ants!" Fonzie called after him.

"Boy, Fonz, you're going to be on TV!" Ralph said, when Howard had gone.

"Yeah, this store is gonna be jammed!" Fonzie said.

"You'll really pull in the customers, huh?" Ralph said.

"Customers? I'm talking about dames. Once The Fonz is on TV, this joint is gonna be crammed with dolls with autograph books and sneaky intentions. How am I gonna get any work done?"

"I'll handle the girls for you, Fonz," Ralph said.

"I'll help, too," Potsie said eagerly.

"It won't work," Fonzie replied, starting on the rebuilding of a bike. "When a dame goes to a bakery for a cheese cake, she's after cream cheese, not Limburger."

Asisted by Richie, Potsie, and Ralph, Fonzie was completing the rebuilding of the first bike the next day, when a young man in Jodhpurs and riding boots and carrying a riding crop entered the shop.

"There must be a plague," Fonzie said. "Everybody's horse is dying."

"I have never *had* a horse," the young man said testily. "Horses make me sneeze. I am Lance Hospice, of the advertising agency Hospice, Rankle & Grosse." He looked distastefully around the shop. "I am here to make a silk purse out of a sow's ear," he said.

"It's somebody for you," Fonzie said to Ralph.

"No, Fonz," Richie said, "he must be here to make the TV commercial."

"Precisely," Lance Hospice said, as an older man

entered with a television camera. "My film crew," he said.

"All one of him?" Fonzie asked.

"He moves around a lot, giving the impression of a multitude," Hospice said. "That's the essence of communications, you know—the impression that is conveyed. No one really looks at or listens to a television commercial. Heavens! If we did, we'd all have ache-aches in our tum-tums, wouldn't we? What the viewer gets is the shadow, not the substance."

Fonzie turned to Richie. "Cunningham, what's he saying?"

"I don't know."

"As long as I understand, it isn't necessary for you to understand," Hospice told them. "Just cooperate."

"Yeah, I have the feeling that if I understood, I'd have a pain-pain in the seat of my pants-pants," Fonzie said.

The film crew was bringing in the lights. He was followed through the doorway by Howard Cunningham.

"Good—the shooting hasn't started yet," Howard said. "Is the bike rebuilt?" he asked Fonzie.

"As good as I can do it," Fonzie replied. "When you're putting together a silk purse, it don't help when the pig is deaf."

Howard stared at him, baffled. "What?"

"The sow's ear wasn't the best, Dad," Richie explained.

Howard turned the stare on his son. "What?"

"This bike we rebuilt wasn't much to begin with," Fonzie told him. "It's the kind of bike that, if I was buying a bike, I wouldn't even give it a first look."

"Oh. Well, that's all right. No matter what you say, it will be believable. You're The Fonz."

"Can we begin?" Hospice said impatiently. "From here, I'm going for cocktails with a really important client."

"Do we have time for one rehearsal?" Howard asked.

Hospice sighed drearily. "Oh, I suppose so."

"Go ahead, Fonzie, say what you're going to say," Howard said.

Fonzie faced the camera. "Heyyyyyyy!" he said. "This is The Fonz. I got—"

"No, no, no, no, no!" Hospice said crankily. "Not 'The Fonz.' That's much too . . . too . . . too hostile . . . Call yourself Friendly Fonzie. The viewers want you to be friendly. You're the only friend they have. If they had any other friends, they wouldn't be sitting around watching television. They'd be having cocktails with their friends, wouldn't they?"

"But there's already a Friendly in the used bike business," Howard said. "Friendly Foster."

"Is his business successful?"

"I suppose so," Howard replied.

"Well, you see? It's because the viewers look upon him as a friend. Believe me, they need friends, they crave friends. They're a miserable lot." He faced Fonzie again. "You're Friendly Fonzie," he said.

"I'm The Fonz," Fonzie replied.

"He's The Fonz," Richie told Hospice.

"He's The Fonz, all right," Potsie said.

"The Fonz," Ralph said.

Hospice turned away in disgust. "I won't be responsible."

"Start again, Fonzie," Howard said.

Once more, Fonzie faced the camera. "Heyyyyyy!" he said. "This is The Fonz! I got this new used bike store. It used to be a bakery, so when you come in, don't step on the ants."

Hospice groaned.

"Right now, just starting up in business," Fonzie continued, "I only got one bike for sale—and it's no bargain, believe me. But, if you don't care what you ride around town on—"

"No!" Hospice cried out. "Oh, no, no, no!" He was near tears. "You can't say that to the viewers!"

"It's the truth," Fonzie told him.

"Truth? If they wanted truth, they'd be at a foreign movie, not watching television! They want illusion! They want the Biggest! They want the Best! They want their dreams to come true! In short, they want lies! Lies! Lies! Lies! Do you understand? Lies!"

"The Fonz don't lie to nobody," Fonzie replied. "The Fonz calls a sow's ear a sow's ear."

"Of course, of course," Hospice said. "That's why I want you to call yourself Friendly Fonzie. Don't you see? That way, it won't be The Fonz lying, it will be somebody named Friendly Fonzie. That makes it all right."

"Fonzie," Howard said, "he's the expert. At least *try* it his way."

"What do you want me to say?" Fonzie asked Hospice.

"Describe the shiny paint job. Talk about how the headlight goes on and off when you flick that little button. Point out that the handlebar grips are made of *real* rubber. Then talk about the joys of biking. Tell them that owning a used bike makes all men handsome and all women beautiful. Tell them that a used bike cures corns, warts, migraine headaches, arthritis, and fleas."

"Fleas?" Howard asked.

"It never hurts to play to the dog-owners," Hospice explained.

Fonzie addressed Howard. "Send this nerd back to Hospital, Crinkle, and Gropes," he said. "I'm not saying that stuff."

"That's Hospice, Rankle & Grosse," Hospice said indignantly. "And I resign the account!"

"Now, wait—" Howard began.

"No, I'm sorry," Hospice said, heading for the door. "I refuse to compromise my integrity! It's lies or nothing!" He stalked out.

The camera crew began taking down the lights that he had set up.

"Hold it!" Fonzie said to the man. "We don't need that nerd from Hotchkiss, Tinkle & Mopes. We can shoot our own TV commercial. Turn on your camera. I'll do the rest."

"Fonzie, I don't think—" Howard began.

"You don't need to think, that's what I'm here for," Fonzie told him. "You just handle the profits when they roll in."

"So far—"

"You're on!" the camera crew said to Fonzie.

Fonzie faced the camera again. "Heyyyyyyyy! This is The Fonz! I got this new used bike store. It's called the Biketeria, on account of it's not a bakery any more—so don't let the ants bother you. Now, before I show you the bike I got for sale, I want to tell you that later we hope to have some *good* merchandise. This particular bike, however, is something else. In the first place—"

Howard headed for the door. "I can't listen!" he said. "That's *my* investment he's shoving down a manhole."

"Rat hole," Richie said faintly, as his father hustled out.

Several days later, in the evening, when the Biketeria commercial was scheduled to make its first appearance on television, the Cunninghams and Fonzie gathered around the set. The Mickey Mouse Club—the program that the spot was to follow—was not yet over.

"I forget," Marion said, peering at the screen, "which one is Mickey?"

"Those are children," Howard told her.

"But those ears—"

"Hats, Marion," Howard said.

"I thought they were a little strange for mice," Marion said.

"Yes, you rarely see mice that sing and tap dance."

"No, I mean none of them has whiskers," Marion said.

"They probably make them shave," Fonzie said. "The kids that watch this show try to be like the Mouseketeers, you know. And what parents want their kids going around with beards."

"That would be unfortunate," Howard agreed.

"Worse than that," Fonzie said. "You'd have kids all over the country dragging their beards through their cornflakes."

"Oh, what a nice song," Marion said, her attention on the screen again.

Fonzie sang along. ". . . Emm . . . Eye . . . Cee . . .

See you real soon . . . Kay . . . Eee . . . Wye . . . Why? Because it's in my contract . . ."

The program ended and a toy commercial came on.

"You'll be next, Fonz," Richie said.

"Heyyy! That's a great toy! We never had dynamite kits that could blow up a whole building when I was a kid. The best ours would do was maybe blow out a few windows."

"Progress," Howard commented.

A cereal commercial came on.

"You'll be next, Fonz," Richie said.

"It shouts 'Help! I'm drowning!' when you pour milk on it?" Fonzie said, watching the cereal commercial.

"More progress," Howard said. "In the old days, the most cereal could do was mutter 'snap, crackle, pop.' "

"Maybe it was telling us it was drowning but we just didn't understand it," Marion said. "I always suspected that there was more to 'snap, crackle, pop' than we realized."

A candy bar commercial came on next.

"Yeah, Cunningham, I know—I'm next," Fonzie said.

"Oh, isn't that cute how the alligator is machine-gunning all those squirrels to get their Fudgie-Nut Crunch bars away from them," Marion said. She frowned. "I didn't know alligators liked candy bars that much."

"They don't," Fonzie said. "But they're nuts about machine-gunning."

An insecticide commercial came on.

"Hey, I think they went past me," Fonzie said. "Listen, if the spot for the Biketeria ever comes on, give me a yell. I'll be up in my room," he said, leaving.

"No, wait, Fonz!" Richie said. "You're bound to be next!"

Reluctantly, Fonzie lingered. "That's the first time I ever saw a mosquito fly an airplane," he said, looking at the screen. "Hey! Anti-aircraft fire!"

"That's the insecticide," Howard said.

"It explodes like that? Shrapnel and everything?"

"Not in real life," Marion said. "In real life, it blows back into your eyes."

The commercial for the Biketeria came on.

Howard clapped his hands over his ears. "I can't listen!"

"Fonzie, you look wonderful!" Joanie said.

"What'd you expect? It's The Fonz, isn't it?"

On the screen, Fonzie was pointing to the bike's motor. "The only thing the matter with this is, when you put a new engine in, you got to put in the same kind as the old engine," he said. "The company that makes the bike works it that way so they can keep selling you junk. This engine, as an engine, would make somebody a good egg beater."

"You have nice eyes on television, Arthur," Marion said. "The eyes are windows to the soul."

"Yeah, I can make my eyelids go up and down like window shades," Fonzie said.

On the screen, Fonzie faced directly into the camera. "So, here's the deal," he said. "It was a lousy bike to start with. But I didn't make it any worse. If you want to buy it, I got a partner who will take your money."

A commercial for a do-it-yourself cesspool kit came on.

Richie turned off the set.

There was silence.

Finally, Marion spoke. "On the other hand, it wasn't like all the other commercials," she said.

"It wasn't like any commercial that has ever been or ever will be," Howard said glumly. "It was a complete waste of money. It was even worse than that. We would have done more good for ourselves if we'd paid the television station *not* to run that commercial."

"Come on, now, enough of this soft soap," Fonzie said. "Tell me what you really thought of it."

"Catastrophe!" Howard said.

"It could have used an alligator," Joanie said. "Even a machine gun might have helped."

"I would have liked it," Marion said, "if you'd just used your eyes and left out the part about the motorcycle."

Fonzie turned to Richie. "Cunningham?"

"Promise you won't hit me, Fonz?"

"I won't hit you. What'd you think of the commercial?"

"Well, it was awful."

"Yeah, but great awful or only good awful?"

The phone rang.

"That's probably some nerd calling to add insult to insult," Fonzie said disgustedly.

Howard picked up the receiver and identified himself, then began a conversation. "Yes . . . the Biketeria? . . . Are you sure you mean the Biketeria? . . . yes . . . Is this a joke? . . . Yes, I remember you . . . The Policemen's Ball . . . Yes, we had a lovely time . . . When you say 'riot,' do you actually mean a riot?

... Oh, I see, any number under ten is loitering and any number over ten is a riot ... Yes, of course we will ... Yes, you can pencil me in for two tickets to next year's Policemen's Ball, too ... Yes, thank you ..." Howard hung up.

"I know ... send your tuxedo out to be cleaned," Marion said.

"Yes, that," Howard said. "But—" He was unable to continue speaking for a second. "That was Sergeant McWorter of the Police Department," he said. "There's a riot at the Biketeria."

Fonzie threw up his hands. "Okay, I'm convinced— it was a lousy commercial. "No! No, it wasn't," it was a lousy commercial.

"No! No, it wasn't," Howard said. "Those are customers who are rioting. They're rioting because they want to buy that bike you advertised on TV and the store is closed." Recovering from the shock, he jumped up. "We've got to get down there to the store and stop them!" he said. "I promised the Sergeant!"

"We'll take my bike—that's the fastest way," Fonzie said, heading for the door.

"Howard, make the police help you stop the riot," Marion called after her husband, as he hurried after Fonzie. "Buy four Ball tickets if you have to!"

Outside, Fonzie started his bike and Howard got on behind him and they roared off in the direction of the Biketeria.

"Not so fast!" Howard shouted over the noise of the motorcycle.

"I can't hear you!"

"I said 'Not so fast!'"

"I can't go no faster!" Fonzie answered.

"Not faster! Slower! Go slower!"

"I can't hear you!"

"Stop!" Howard pleaded.

"That's where we're going—the shop!"

"Not the shop! Stop! Halt!"

"Who's got time for a malt? There's a riot!"

Howard gave up. He settled for closing his eyes.

A few minutes later, they reached the Biketeria. There was a crowd at the entrance, being held back by a squad of uniformed policemen. At the sight of Fonzie, the crowd began swarming toward his bike. The police moved quickly to protect Fonzie and Howard, surrounding them, keeping the crowd at a distance. The people in the crowd began chanting: "Buy! Buy! Buy! Buy! Buy!"

"Sergeant McWorter," one of the policemen said, approaching Howard and Fonzie. He got out a book of tickets. "Two, was it?" he said. "Won't you boys want a couple tickets for your wives, also?"

"Sergeant, this is hardly the time for that!" Howard said. "That mob is wild!"

"That's no mob," McWorter said. "That's just a typical bunch of shoppers, looking for a bargain. They got bedazzled by your TV ad. I saw it myself and almost got took in. How often do you see an honest advertisement? Then I realized—it was just a new gimmick." He nodded toward the crowd. "They're not as smart as us officers of the law."

"What do we do now?" Howard asked.

"Open your doors and sell your bikes," McWorter replied.

"But we only have one bike to sell," Howard told him. "And there must be at least fifty people in that crowd."

"Then, it's first come, first served," McWorter said. He got a bull horn from another policeman and addressed the crowd. "There's only one bike—the one you seen on TV. So, by order of the authority invested in me by his honor, the Mayor, I'm declaring this a state of emergency. That means that what I say goes. And what I say goes is, the bike goes to the first one that showed up here tonight. Will that lucky person please raise his hand, unless he's a she!"

Fifty hands went up.

"Well, I tried my best," McWorter said to Howard. "It's your can of beans now. I hope you can talk yourself out of it without getting killed."

"Give me that squawker," Fonzie said.

The Sergeant handed him the bull horn.

"Heyyyy!" Fonzie said to the crowd. "This is The Fonz!"

They cheered.

"Don't try to get on the good side of me with all that rah-rah," Fonzie said. "You're acting like a bunch of nerds. Now, right now, we got one bike. Later, if a lot of guys get careless and wreck up their machines, we'll have more. But now is now and later is some other time."

"Who gets the bike?" someone yelled from the crowd.

"I'm getting to that. I was honest with you on the TV," Fonzie said, still speaking through the bull horn, "so now it's your turn to be honest with me. Honest— who was here first?"

Twenty-five hands went up.

"That's the crookedest honest since the last time

that question was asked," Fonzie told them. "Try again."

"Ten hands went up."

"Heyyyyyy! You all want a rap in the mouth!"

At last, only one hand went up.

"I'm proud of you," Fonzie said. "A lot of mobs would let themselves get beat up before they turned honest. Okay, the winner can stay. The rest of you, go home. And don't come back till we get more wrecked bikes to sell!"

The crowd began dispersing.

"You're lucky to be a civilian," McWorter said to Fonzie. "If us cops threaten a mob with a rap in the mouth, we lose our siren privileges for a month."

When the crowd had gone, Fonzie opened the store and he and Howard and McWorter escorted the young man who had won the right to buy the bike inside.

"That's it," Fonzie said, gesturing toward the motorcycle.

"Wow!" the young man said, rubbing his hands together gleefully. "All mine! How much?" he asked Fonzie.

Fonzie shrugged. "What can you afford?"

"Five-hundred dollars?"

"That's the price!" Howard said quickly.

"Heyyy! That's too much!" Fonzie said. "That bike's not worth no five-hundred clams."

"Four-fifty," the young man said.

"Sold!" Howard said.

"Nah, too high," Fonzie said. "Try two-fifty," he said to the young man.

"Two-fifty?"

"You're getting warm," Fonzie said.

"Two-hundred?"

"Right on the button," Fonzie told him. "That is a two-hundred clam bike. Pay the cashier," he said, indicating Howard.

The young man got a wad of bills from his pocket and began peeling tens from it and handing them to Howard. His hands trembled. "I'm so nervous," he said. "This is the first time in my life I ever got exactly what I paid for."

"Tell your friends where it happened," Howard said. "We can use all the word-of-mouth advertising we can get."

"Friends?" the young man said, putting the final ten dollar bill into Howard's hands. "If I had any friends, would I have been watching TV? The Mickey Mouse Club?" He wheeled the bike toward the exit.

"Wait a minute!" Howard called after him. "One of these tens has been chewed on."

"Oh . . . that's my dog's contribution," the young man replied, leaving. "He thinks this bike is going to cure his fleas."

"Clever gimmick," McWorter said to Howard and Fonzie. "And all legal."

"What gimmick?" Howard asked.

"That honesty angle," McWorter replied, as they left the store. "You get a guy in here and he wants to pay five-hundred bucks for a bike and you chisel him down to two-hundred. The general public wouldn't see through it. But when you've been a cop as long as I have, nothing fools you any more."

"Keep it quiet . . . *please!*" Howard said. "If we work that gimmick a few more times, we'll be bankrupt."

"What do you think I am, a tattle-tale?" McWorter said. "As far as I'm concerned, as soon as you buy those six tickets to the Policemen's Ball, the whole thing is forgotten."

"It was two tickets," Howard protested. "Four at the most. I can't—"

The radio in McWorter's car came to life.

"Just a minute," the Sergeant said, hurrying toward the car. "Business before pressure."

Howard and Fonzie trailed after him. When they reached the police car, McWorter was getting in behind the wheel.

"Wreck on the highway," the Sergeant said, starting the engine. "Got to fly!"

"Not a bad wreck, I hope," Howard said, concerned.

"The tree's in pretty bad condition," McWorter replied.

"The tree?"

"A guy on a motorcycle run into it," McWorter said.

The police car sped away, its siren wailing.

"A bike wreck!" Fonzie said.

"Follow that car!" Howard said.

They ran to Fonzie's bike and jumped aboard it and set out in pursuit of the Sergeant.

"Faster!" Howard shouted over the roar of the motorcycle engine.

"I can't hear you!"

"Never mind!" Howard said. He shouted again. "With this kind of hustle, we'll soon be the used bike kings of the country!"

"What?"

"Hustle!" Howard shouted.

"You go nuts on a bike!" Fonzie shouted back. "Last time, you wanted to stop for a malt. Now, you want me to stop and feel your muscle!"

THREE

When Fonzie and Richie arrived at the Biketeria
the next morning, Richie was carrying a set of
ledgers. At his father's request, he was going to start
keeping books on the business, keeping a record of
the money going out and coming in.

Dumped just inside the door was the motorcycle
that had been wrecked on the highway the night before and that Howard and Fonzie had purchased and
brought back to the shop. The bike was hardly recog-
nizable as such. Its wheels were twisted into pretzel-
like shapes. Its frame sagged in the middle, as if it
were the skeleton for a sway-backed horse.

"I heard the ambulance siren last night," Richie
said. "The guy who was on this bike must have really
cracked-up."

"No, he was okay," Fonzie said. "He fell off the
bike before it hit the tree. All he got was some
scratches. That was the tree surgeon's ambulance you
heard. They don't think the tree is going to make it.
All its limbs were broken."

"They took it away in an ambulance?" Richie said.

"To the tree hospital. To put it in traction. But the

tree surgeon said it hasn't got much of a chance. It lost too much sap."

Richie looked down at the wreck again. "How much did you pay for it?"

"It was the other way around," Fonzie replied. "The guy whose bike it was gave us ten bucks to carry it away. He claims it's a bad luck bike. He says it chases trees."

Richie looked at him dubiously.

Like a dog chases cars," Fonzie explained.

"You don't believe that, do you?"

"Who knows? I once had a bike that was drawn to fresh-laid eggs," Fonzie said. "I'd be riding along a country road and all of a sudden, I'd feel the bike drifting. Everytime I gave it its head, it took me to some farmer's hen house. I had to get rid of it. I was broke all the time, keeping it in fresh eggs."

Looking skeptical, Richie sat down on the floor and leaned back against the wall and opened the ledgers. Fonzie, meanwhile, began carrying the parts of the wrecked bike to the back of the shop.

"I guess the ten bucks that guy gave you is profit," Richie said. "But, you didn't sell anything to get it, so maybe it isn't. I wonder what I ought to write it down under?"

"Is there a miscellaneous?" Fonzie asked.

"Yes."

"There's your answer."

"That bike you sold last night for two-hundred dollars," Richie said. "How much did it cost to rebuild it?"

"You want an exact number?"

"I think so."

"A hundred and ninety-nine dollars and thirty cents."

"Fonz, that means you only made seventy-cents profit," Richie said. "Not even that much, counting the cost of your labor. Actually, you lost money on the deal."

"Take the loss out of miscellaneous," Fonzie suggested. "That way, we'll about break even."

"I guess I can do that," Richie decided, revising the ledger.

A large man who was smoking a large cigar and wearing a large western hat entered the store. He halted just inside the doorway and looked about, smiling amiably.

"Heyyy! I know you from somewhere, don't I?" Fonzie said.

"Friendly Foster is the name," the man beamed. "Sunshine is the game."

"Yeah, I saw you on your TV ads."

"And the same to you," Friendly Foster said, sauntering on into the store. "That was a doozy, that ad of yours. Why, you almost had me running over here to buy that bike myself. If there's anything I admire, son, it's a smooth operator. And that honesty twist you put on that ad was smooooooth!"

"It wasn't a twist," Richie told Friendly Foster.

"Call it what you want." He looked around again. "I heard about that riot last night," he said. "Customers stacked ten feet high, they tell me. Too bad you didn't have the merchandise to accommodate them."

"They'll be back when we get some bikes," Fonzie said.

"Don't count on it, son. Customers are fickle. Let

me tell you a little story. When I first started up my store, I had a grand opening sale. The customers loved me for that. But then the next day when I doubled prices, they stopped coming around." He looked away, his expression becoming suddenly hard. "I guess it made me a little bitter." Abruptly, his smile returned. "Then I learned friendliness," he said. "It was just the twist I needed. If it's done in a friendly way, the customers love those double prices."

"To each his own," Fonzie said, separating the parts of the wrecked bike.

"That honesty twist of yours is just a flash in the pan," Friendly said. "Friendliness is what sells. You'll never see those customers again. I give this operation a month—two months at the most—then it'll fold. And I hate to see that," he said. "I *like* competition."

"We'll try to make you happy," Fonzie told him.

"When I say I like competition, I mean I like it in other businesses," Friendly Foster said. "I'm not too fond of it in the used bike business, though. It's not friendly. Why, before you know it, you and me will be at each other's throats. I'll cut prices, you'll cut prices, I'll cut prices further, you'll cut prices even more, and so on and so on and so on. Nobody will be making any money."

"We're not gonna cut prices," Fonzie said.

"You say that now. But wait'll I turn my back. I can feel the knife between my shoulder blades already."

"You want me to sign something that I won't stab you in the back?" Fonzie asked.

"It would only be a piece of paper," Friendly replied. "I know about pieces of paper. I give a guarantee with every used bike I sell. But it's just a piece of paper—worthless. If you want to sign something, though, how about a piece of paper that says I'm the owner of the Biketeria?"

Fonzie and Richie peered at him puzzled.

"I'm offering to buy you out," Friendly Foster said. "I'll give you what you've invested in the business, so far, and a little something that you can call a profit."

"I can't do that. I got a partner," Fonzie told him.

"Who's your partner?"

"My father," Richie said. "Howard Cunningham."

"The hardware store?"

Richie nodded.

"So, Cunningham's out to get me, is he?" Friendly said. He was no longer smiling. "I see what he's do-ing. He wants to run me out of business, then open up a spare parts department in his hardware store! He'll have a monopoly. Every biker in town will have to go to him for parts!"

"No, he's not—" Richie began.

"Don't tell me! It's what I'd do if I had a hardware store," Friendly said. "Well, you can tell him: This is war!"

"But he—"

"War!" Friendly bellowed, striding out. "War! War!"

"It sounds like war to me," Fonzie said, when Friendly Foster had gone.

"Boy, he wasn't very friendly there at the end, was he?"

"He was *kind* of friendly," Fonzie said. "He didn't bomb us. In a war, I think, if the other guy doesn't blow you up, it means that, down deep, he likes you."

From outside came an explosion.

Richie and Fonzie covered their heads.

There was silence.

"It's okay," Fonzie said. "It was only a backfire."

That evening, Richie and Fonzie told Howard about Friendly Foster's visit to the Biketeria and his declaration of war.

"He's bluffing," Howard said.

"He sounded serious," Richie said.

"In times of stress, people make threats that they don't mean," Howard said. "When he got back to his store and cooled off, I'm sure he changed his mind." He switched on the TV set. "Let me relax, will you?" he said. "I had a hard day today. I got in a shipment of drill bits that turned out to be asparagus spears."

"How could that happen?"

"Well .... they look a little alike ... except that asparagus spears are green ..."

A soap powder commercial came on.

"Hey, they're right," Fonzie said, his eyes on the screen. "That woman *was* shorter and fatter and had pimples before she washed her clothes in that stuff."

A commercial for Friendly Foster's came on.

"I wouldn't be seen at a hog-calling contest on this," Friendly Foster said, pointing to a bike. "Look at that paint job. The paint will be peeling before you ever get it out of the store."

"He's stealing our honesty!" Howard said, outraged. "He *did* mean it! This *is* war!"

On the screen, Friendly Foster kicked the bike. "I'm surprised it didn't fall apart," he told the viewers. "We stuck it together with flour-and-water paste. But, if you're sucker enough to buy it, Friendly Foster's is the place to come."

"He didn't steal our honesty," Fonzie said. "He's lying. That's not a bad bike."

"That's even worse," Howard said, fuming. "It's dishonest honesty."

On the screen, Friendly Foster faced straight into the camera. "And now, I'd like to say a word to those bikers who happen to be accident prone," he said. "If you get the feeling that your luck has run out and you're about to crack-up your bike, give Friendly Foster a call. Let Friendly be there when it happens. I pay the highest prices for wrecks."

A commercial for a do-it-yourself tunnel blasting kit came on.

Enraged, Howard switched off the set. "He's stealing our customers!" he said.

"They're not our customers," Fonzie said. "They're anybody's customers."

"They're ours!" Howard insisted. "We thought up honesty first! But he has bikes to sell. By the time he finishes with them, they won't be customers any more!" He sat down heavily in his chair. "We've got to create a new market," he said.

"What're you talking about?" Fonzie asked. "Going out of the bike business and into the asparagus business?"

"No, no, a new market for used bikes," Howard replied. "Who will Friendly Foster be selling to? To bikers, people who already ride bikes. We've got to sell to people who, at present, *don't* ride bikes."

"Nerds?" Fonzie said.

"Not necessarily. Let's think—who doesn't ride bikes?"

"I never seen no new-born baby on a bike," Fonzie

said. "They're legs are too short to reach the kick stand."

"You're on the right track," Howard said.

"New-born babies don't have a lot of money," Fonzie pointed out. "It would fall out of their diapers."

"Me!" Howard said exultantly. "I don't ride a bike!"

"Dad, there isn't going to be much of profit in that," Richie said, "selling your own bikes to yourself."

"Not me. People like me. Middle-aged people. We're a whole new vast untapped market for bikes!" He called out toward the kitchen. "Marion! Come in here!"

"People like you and Mrs. Cunningham riding bikes?" Fonzie said.

"Fonz, what's the matter?" Richie said. "You're turning green."

"Either I'm an asparagus spear or the idea of middle-aged nerds on bikes is giving me a pain-pain in the tum-tum," Fonzie replied. "Middle-agers on bikes is just not cool."

"Yes, dear," Marion said, arriving from the kitchen.

"How would you like to learn to ride a bike?" Howard asked her.

"Why, I already know how, dear. You just push the pedals and that makes the wheels go around. I'm not entirely sure *how* that happens, but I think the wheels are connected in some way to the handlebars."

"I'm gonna lose my dinner," Fonzie said weakly.

"No, not a bicycle, Marion, a motorcycle," Howard said.

The color left Marion's face. "A vroom-vroom motorcycle?"

"Why not?" Howard replied. "Just because we're

middle-aged, that doesn't mean we can't have a little spice in our life. Can't you just see us vroom-vrooming along the highway, leaving our cares behind? Why, it would be like being young again, Marion."

"Well . . ."

"It's settled," Howard said. "That will be our next TV commercial."

"You and Mrs. Cunningham vroom-vrooming along the highway, leaving your cares behind?" Fonzie asked.

"Yes. Other middle-aged people will see the commercial and they'll want to do the same thing. Naturally, they'll come to the Biketeria to buy bikes."

"You know how to ride a bike?" Fonzie asked Howard.

"Not yet." he replied. "You're going to teach us, Marion and me."

Fonzie suddenly turned and rushed from the room.

"Where is he going?" Howard asked puzzledly.

"To lose his dinner, Dad," Richie explained.

When Howard and Marion arrived at the Biketeria the next day, Fonzie had a pair of matched Harley Davidsons waiting for them.

"Those are handsome bikes!" Howard said. "Where did you get them? How did you get them rebuilt so quickly?"

"These bikes have never been wrecked," Fonzie told him. "I borrowed the loan of them from a couple friends of mine. If you're gonna learn to ride a bike, you want to learn on the best. Okay—get aboard."

Howard and Marion mounted the bikes.

"This *is* fun!" Marion said. "Look, Howard! Look in the rear-view mirror. You can see the street behind us." She looked more closely at the mirror. "The Bon Ton Dress Shoppe is having a sale."

"Marion, forget the sale. Pay attention to the instructions."

"This," Fonzie said, "is the ignition—or, to be technical, how you turn it on."

"It's darling," Marion said.

"Now, right here, this is your accelerator," Fonzie said, continuing.

"I wonder if the Bon Ton still has that brown knit," Marion said. "It was too expensive last week, but on sale—"

"Marion, please. Listen to what Fonzie is telling us."

"Oh, yes—I'm sorry."

"Here is your gear," Fonzie said. "Right now, it's in neutral. When it's in neutral, you don't go no place."

"This is simpler than I expected," Howard said. "It's just like a car."

Fonzie pointed to the ignition switch. "Now, what is this?"

"The brake?" Marion guessed.

"I haven't even mentioned the brakes yet."

"Well, something has to be the brake," Marion said defensively.

"Okay, both together, try your ignitions," Fonzie said.

Howard and Marion switched on the motors.

"Heyyyyy! You got it!" Fonzie said, amazed. "Now, all you got to do—" He interrupted himself, staring up the street.

Howard and Marion looked in the same direction. A beautiful, slender, dark-haired girl was approaching the Biketeria. She appeared to be gliding along rather than walking, so smooth were her movements. As pedestrians passed her, they looked back, awed. She looked as if she had stepped from the cover of some ultra-chic fashion magazine.

"Heyyyyyyyyyyy!" Fonzie said.

"She must be lost, poor thing," Marion said.

"Why do you say that?" Howard asked.

"Why would anyone as beautiful as she is be in Milwaukee on purpose?"

Reaching them, the girl halted. "I'm Magda," she said. "I'm a stranger in town." Her voice was a throaty purr. "Are you . . . The Fonz?" she asked.

"I was," Fonzie replied. "Let me check. Yeah . . . I'm The Fonz."

"I saw you on television," Magda said. Her expression became seductive. "I want to . . . want to . . . I want to learn from you . . ."

"Yiiii!" Fonzie said.

"First, of course, I'll need a bike," Magda said.

"You got more to learn than you think," Fonzie told her. "A bike is not necessary."

She seemed perplexed. "How can I learn to ride a bike if I don't *have* a bike?"

"Oh, a bike!" Fonzie said. "You want to learn how to ride a bike! When you said learn, I thought you were talking about my specialty—which no bike is needed for, unless you happen to be a little kinky."

"Do you *have* a bike for me?" Magda purred.

"The only bike I got at the moment is in about a hundred different pieces," Fonzie replied.

"Could I . . . look at it?" Magda asked huskily.

"Yeah. Only, at the moment, I happen to be giving a lesson on riding to a couple middle-aged—"

"That's all right, Fonzie," Howard said. "The customers come first. We'll stay here and think about what we've learned so far."

"Just don't get ahead of the lesson," Fonzie warned.

"Fonzie, we're not children. We won't do anything we're not supposed to do."

Fonzie led the way into the shop, with Magda slinking after him.

"What town are you not a stranger in?" he asked.

"Quite a few. New York, San Francisco, Chicago, Hong Kong—"

"Hong Kong? Did they turn that ape into a town?"

"You're thinking of King Kong," Magda said. "Hong Kong is in China." She looked at him steamily. "I'm a missionary's daughter," she said. "Daddy and I saved souls . . . he in his way . . . and me in mine . . ."

"I bet your old man didn't get a lot of business," Fonzie said. He pointed to the collection of parts on the floor that had once been a motorcycle. "There it is. How do you like it so far?"

"It reminds me of some of the souls I saved . . . strung out . . ."

"Yeah. Well, it'll be a couple days before I get it strung back together," Fonzie said. "But, in the meantime, I got a bike of my own I can teach you on. Have you ever—"

From outside came the sudden roar of an engine.

"Marion! No!" Howard was heard crying.

There was a second roar.

"I think the children are doing something they're not supposed to," Fonzie said, hurrying toward the door.

Magda followed quickly after him.

When they reached the sidewalk, they saw the twin bikes with Howard and Marion aboard racing up the street. Marion was hanging on precariously. Howard was waving wildly with one hand, as if by getting her attention he could somehow bring her bike to a halt.

Fonzie jumped onto his bike. "Excuse me," he said to Magda. "I got a couple souls to save myself."

"What about my lesson?"

"Hop on back! Just one rule: no backseat driving!"

Magda got on the bike behind him.

"This is the starter," Fonzie told her, switching on the motor. "And that was the gear, and that was the accelerator," he called back to her as the bike shot forward and raced up the street.

Ahead, Marion was still in the lead, and Howard was still waving wildly.

"We don't seem to be gaining," Magda shouted to Fonzie.

"I can't hear you!"

"We're not gaining!"

Fonzie held out a hand, palm up, and looked up at the sky.

"Not raining! Gaining!"

"Yeah, they're gaining. They must have it wide-open!"

Ahead, Marion swerved onto the sidewalk, scattering pedestrians. A moment later, her bike left the sidewalk and nearly collided with Howard's bike, which was still in the street. For a second, they rode side by side. Then Marion's bike veered off again and bounced over the curb and onto the opposite sidewalk, sending pedestrians diving for safety once more.

"She's out of control!" Magda shouted to Fonzie.

"Over here, we call it gas, not petrol," he shouted back, "and she's got a whole tank full."

"Not— Oh, never mind!"

"I can't hear you!"

"Never mind!"

"Behind? That's Howard Cunningham. He's my partner."

From the rear came the wail of a siren, then a police car pulled up beside Fonzie's bike. Sergeant McWorter was at the wheel.

"You're speeding!" McWorter yelled to Fonzie. "Pull over! I'm going to sell you a ticket!"

Fonzie pointed ahead. "Runaway bikes!"

"Riding a motorcycle on the sidewalk!" McWorter said, peering through his windshield. "That'll cost them ten tickets at the very least!"

"We got to do something!" Fonzie shouted to him. "They don't know how to stop those bikes!"

"I'll get on the radio and set up a roadblock," McWorter answered.

Ahead, Marion left the sidewalk and joined Howard in the street again. They dodged in and out among the cars. Zooming through a traffic signal, they had cars swerving in all directions to avoid hitting them.

"Emergency!" McWorter said into his radio microphone. "Two prospects for tickets to the Ball heading east on runaway motorcycles! Set up a road block at the city line! Bring plenty of books of tickets!"

"We're getting to the edge of town, I think!" Magda shouted to Fonzie.

"I can't hear you!"

"Edge of town!"

"Milwaukee!" Fonzie shouted back.

"I know what town it is. I—"

"I can't hear you!" McWorter shouted over to her.

"I said I know it's Milwaukee!"

"We'd all be safer walking!" McWorter shouted back, agreeing.

Ahead, the runaway bikes left the city street, following a ramp that would take them to the highway.

"They're headed for the roadblock!" McWorter called out to Fonzie. "It's all over now but the terrible carnage when they ram into those police cars!"

"Get your police cars out of there!" Fonzie shouted to him. "Those are borrowed bikes!"

"Too late!"

Fonzie and Magda on Fonzie's bike and McWorter in the police car turned onto the ramp. Ahead, Howard and Marion reached the highway—and shot straight across it and leaped a drainage ditch and landed in a pasture and kept on going.

"Not that way!" McWorter shouted. He pointed in the direction of the highway. "That way to the carnage!"

Howard's and Marion's bikes plowed into a hay stack. The bikes came out the other side—but Howard and Marion did not. Roaring on, riderless, the bikes crashed into a barn. The air was filled with flying parts.

Stopping at the side of the highway, Fonzie and Magda dismounted from Fonzie's bike and McWorter got out of his police car and they ran across the pasture toward the haystack. As they neared it, Howard came staggering out. A moment later, Marion's head emerged from the hay and she peered around dazedly.

"You're alive!" Fonzie said, as he and Magda and McWorter reached the haystack.

Howard blinked at him. "Do I know you?"

"It's me—The Fonz!"

"About those tickets," McWorter said to Howard.

"Riding a motorcycle on a sidewalk, that'll cost you ten. Riding a motorcycle through a red light, that's five more. Riding a motorcycle in an east-west direction on a north-south highway, that's another ten—"

"Marion!" Howard said, in sudden panic. "Where is Marion?"

"I know someone named Marion," Marion said, climbing out of the hay. "She's either my sister or me ... one of us is named Marion."

Howard threw his arms around McWorter. "You're safe!"

"Mr. Cunningham, you're still a little dizzy, I think," Fonzie said. "You got the wrong person for a wife there."

"And I already got a date for the ball," McWorter said.

At that moment, a motorcycle came racing toward them, bounding across the pasture. A second later, the motorcycle skidded to a halt. Friendly Foster jumped off.

"Hello, stranger in town," he said to Magda. Then he faced the others. "Where is the roadblock? Where are the wrecked bikes?"

"How did you know about it?" Fonzie asked.

"I monitor police calls. Where are those— There they are!" he cried out, spotting the wrecked bikes. "I'll pay ten dollars for the two of them!" he said to Howard.

"Twenty!" Fonzie countered.

"Thirty—and that's my last offer!" Friendly Foster told Howard.

"Thirty-five!" Fonzie bid.

"Fifty—and that's really my last offer," Foster said.

"I can't meet that," Fonzie said.

"Sold to—" Howard began.

"Hold it!" Fonzie exploded. "What's going on here! Those aren't your bikes!" he told Howard. "I borrowed the loan of those bikes!"

"I got carried away," Howard said apologetically.

"Curses!" Friendly Foster said. He jumped back aboard his bike. "Wait till the next catastrophe!" he shouted, roaring off. "Friendly Foster *über alles!*"

"What does that mean?" Marion asked.

"I think it's German for 'faster than a speeding bullet,' " McWorter said. "Wasn't that Superman?"

"That was a nut!" Fonzie said. "We're *all* a bunch of nuts! I'm the biggest nut of all! Did you hear me?" he said to Howard. "I was bidding on those bikes! Those bikes that I borrowed. What's happened to me? I'm not The Fonz!"

"You're a businessman now!" Howard told him, delighted. "You're full of the old gee whiz, the old get up and go! You're a world-beater!"

Fonzie turned away, disappearing behind the haystack.

"He's losing his dinner again," Marion said.

FOUR

At the back of the Biketeria, Richie, Potsie, Ralph, and Fonzie were sorting through the parts that had once been a matched pair of Harley Davidsons, dividing them into two piles.

"Were your friends mad when you told them Mr. and Mrs. Cunningham wrecked their bikes?" Potsie asked Fonzie.

"Only until I told them we'd pay them what the bikes cost when they were new," Fonzie replied. "That took a lot of the heartbreak out of it. They said when they get tired of the new bikes they're gonna buy with the money, they'll bring them around and let Mr. and Mrs. Cunningham learn to ride on them. I think they think they've got a good thing going."

"What is this?" Ralph asked, holding up a part.

"That is the backrest off the seat off a tractor," Fonzie replied. "The bike parts got mixed up with some of the junk lying around that barn the bikes ran into."

"I still don't understand how the accident happened," Potsie said. "Weren't you watching Mr. and Mrs. Cunningham, Fonzie?"

"They were outside, sitting on the bikes," Richie

told Potsie, "and Fonzie was inside, with a customer."

"Yeah, I only got as far as teaching the Cunninghams how to switch on the engines," Fonzie said. "Then, while I was inside with the customer, Mrs. Cunningham decided she wanted to turn her engine off and go to a dress sale."

"Only, what she actually did was shift into gear," Richie said.

"And when she went shooting off up the street, Mr. Cunningham, the John Wayne of Milwaukee, had to go riding off to the rescue," Fonzie said. "The rest is haystackery."

"But you didn't have any bikes to sell," Ralph said to Fonzie. "What were you doing inside with a customer?"

"Lining her up for a future sale," Fonzie replied. "Also, I thought I might sell her a bike later on."

As one, Richie, Potsie, and Ralph looked puzzled.

"Fonz, I don't understand that," Richie said.

"What I had in mind first was selling myself," Fonzie told them. "To understand *that*, you had to be there. She was the coolest customer I have ever met in my whole couple weeks in the used bike business."

"Cool how?" Potsie asked.

"You know that movie where Lauren Bacall asks Humphrey Bogart if he knows how to whistle? Cool like that."

"Bacall or Bogart?" Ralph asked.

At that moment, Magda appeared at the entrance.

"Figure it out for yourself," Fonzie replied to Ralph, looking toward the doorway. "Is that the whistl-er or the whistl-ee?"

Turning, Ralph, Richie, and Potsie saw Magda. They stared, awed.

"I'm here for my . . . lesson . . ." Magda said throatily to Fonzie.

He introduced her to Richie, Potsie, and Ralph. "Say something to them in Hong Kong," he said.

"Gong," she purred.

"Hey—that rings a bell," Fonzie said. "I must know some Hong Kong myself." He headed for the doorway, trailed by Richie, Potsie and Ralph, who were still staring at Magda in speechless wonder. "The bike is outside," he said. "I don't keep it in here so no nerd will come along and buy it off me."

"It must be very . . . special to you . . ." Magda said, as they left the shop. "I admire that in a man . . . when he has a very *special* relationship . . . with his machine . . ."

"Wow!" Ralph said, as he and Richie and Potsie halted in the doorway. "Did you hear that? The way she said 'machine?' That's the way Lauren Bacall said 'whistle.' "

"Anything she'd say would sound sexy," Ralph said. "She *is* sexy."

"You never know," Richie said. "With beautiful girls, sometimes, there's less to what they say than meets the ears."

Fonzie and Magda had reached the motorcycle.

"The first rule is, before you can ride a bike, you got to get on it," Fonzie said. "Remember how yesterday you hopped on back? Today, you do the same thing, only you do it up front."

Magda approached the front wheel.

"No, the front of the seat, not the front of the bike," Fonzie told her.

"Beautiful but dumb," Potsie said to Richie and Ralph.

"She doesn't look dumb," Ralph said.

"She doesn't sound dumb," Richie said.

"Maybe it's the language difference," Potsie conceded. "'Front' might mean something different in Hong Kong that it does in English."

At the motorcycle, Magda was now trying to board it from the back.

"Heyyyyyy!" Fonzie said. "This isn't leapfrog! You get on from the side. You put a leg over. You know what legs are, don't you? That's what, when you're walking along the street, guys gawk at you and say, 'Heyyyyyy! What legs!'"

"You know *every*thing, don't you?" Magda said admiringly. "Motorcycles ... legs ... leapfrog ... There must be no end to your store of knowledge. A woman could learn so many, many things from you ..." she said sultrily.

"She could if she'd pay attention," Fonzie agreed. He pointed. "Now, that is the right leg. If you're right-legged, you stand on the left and put the right leg over. Or, if you're vice-versa, you stand on the right and put—" He pointed again. "We're gonna call this other one over here the left leg. You can tell it's the left leg because it's not the right leg. Have you got that—the right leg and the left leg?"

"Of course," she purred. "*This* . . . is the right leg . . ."

"Amen!"

"—and *this* . . . is the left leg . . ." She looked suddenly perplexed. "But what if I turn around?" she asked. "Will the left leg be on the right and the right leg be on the left?"

Fonzie thought for a moment. "Look, let's do it this way," he said. "I'll get a couple barrels and you can stand on them and I'll wheel the bike under you. That's the *only* way you're ever gonna get on this bike."

She pouted. "You're angry with Magda ..."

"Who's angry?" Fonzie replied. "If I was mad, I'd make you get your own barrels. Let's try it again. You stand on the left side of the bike, right where you are, and you take your right leg—"

He was interrupted by the arrival of Howard Cunningham.

"What's everybody doing out here?" Howard asked. "You're supposed to be rebuilding those wrecked bikes we bought yesterday."

"I'm giving the lady a lesson," Fonzie replied. "How am I going to sell her a bike if first she don't learn how to ride?"

"How are you going to sell her a bike if first we don't have any bikes to sell?" Howard countered. "Fonzie, we've got to think of our investment. And when I say 'our' investment, I mean my investment. I have a lot of money tied up in those wrecks. I can't get the money back until the bikes are rebuilt and sold."

"You won't even get it back then, Dad," Richie said. "You paid more for the bikes than you'll ever sell them for."

"But that's because your mother and I wrecked them and I felt responsible," Howard said. "What I'm talking about, in a general way, is how a successful business is operated. You've got to keep your nose to the grindstone. When there is work to be done, you've got to do it. There is a time for work—" He glanced at Magda. "—and a time for play."

"You're right," Fonzie said. "But I think you got it a

little wrong. It's play first and work when you got
nothing else to do. Remember the story of the ant and
the grasshopper?"

"Yes," Howard replied. "The ant put food away for
winter and the grasshopper didn't. And when winter
came—"

"The grasshopper went to Miami," Fonzie said.

"Barbados," Magda said.

The others looked at her questioningly.

"In my set ... the grasshoppers go to Barbados,"
she explained.

"Okay, okay, we'll get to work," Fonzie said to
Howard. He faced Magda again. "I got to put off the
lesson," he said. "My partner is getting heartburn
from his money—which somebody else now has on account of his wife tried to switch off an engine by
shifting it into gear so she could go buy a dress. I'll
tell you what we'll do, though," he continued.
"Tonight, after the sun goes down, I'll come over to
your place and we'll start again at the beginning."

"Legs," Ralph said.

The others looked at him.

"That's the beginning, where you're going to start
again, with the legs," Ralph explained.

"Wherever," Fonzie said. He turned to Howard.
"Are you satisfied? What started with legs, you have
now turned into a day of sweat and toil. Are you
happy?"

"Actually, that wasn't what I had in mind When I
came over here," Howard replied. "I was thinking
ahead. We need more wrecks."

"What do you want me to do, go out and wreck
bikes on my lunch hour?" Fonzie asked.

"He could be arrested for that, Dad," Richie pointed out.

"I don't want *him* to wreck bikes," Howard said. "But something has to be done. Bike riders aren't wrecking their bikes fast enough. We have to do something to help them along."

"How about going around and loosening all their front wheels," Ralph suggested.

Howard winced. "That would be terrible. When I said we have to do something, I meant we have to do something without doing anything."

"We're halfway there," Fonzie said. "Right now, we're not doing anything."

"What I mean is, we have to do something that will naturally result in more wrecks," Howard said. "Loose front wheels is not something that would happen naturally. Also, we don't want anybody to be hurt in these wrecks that happen naturally," he added.

"I think I got it," Fonzie said. "What we do is talk the government into making all the highways out of marshmallow from now on. A guy is riding his bike down this marshmallow highway, see, and his front wheel sticks in the goo, and he gets thrown off. But, it's okay because he lands in the soft marshmallow."

"You've got the right idea," Howard said, "but I don't like bringing the government into it. Too much red tape."

"How about a contest?" Ralph suggested.

"Yeah—a bathing beauty contest!" Potsie said. "I vote for you," he said to Magda. "In fact, I'll vote for you twice—once for your left leg and once for your right leg."

"How juvenile," she said icily.

"Hold it! What good is a bathing beauty contest going to do?" Fonzie said. "What's the prize? For the dame who wins it, we go out and bust up her boyfriend's bike?"

"That wasn't the kind of contest I meant," Ralph said. "I was thinking about, maybe, a trick riding contest."

"Hey, maybe he's got something there," Fonzie said. "Any trick riding contest I ever seen, there was always a lot of wrecked bikes. And nobody ever got hurt bad . . . a few scratches, a couple bruises . . ."

"That's it!" Howard said. "The Biketeria will sponsor a trick riding contest! And every rider who enters it will have to sign a paper giving us custody of his bike if it gets wrecked. We'll pay for the wrecks, of course."

"We'll have to give a prize to the winner," Richie said. "It seems to me that all we've thought up is another way to spend money, buying wrecks and giving prizes."

"Every new business starts that way, Richie," Howard said. "You spend money at first, but, in the end—if you're successful—your money comes back to you, and it brings more money with it. Let's see," he said, continuing, "what kind of prize could we offer that would attract a lot of bikers?"

Potsie glanced at Magda again.

"How juvenile," she said.

"I was thinking about you going out on a date with the winner," he said.

"I am not a piece of liver, to be tossed to the dogs," she told him coldly.

"Hey—cool!" Fonzie said. "Did you hear that? She's not a piece of liver! That's cool! Did you ever hear any girl in Milwaukee say she wasn't no piece of liver? You got to go out-of-state to hear talk like that! That is *cool*!"

"The prize, the prize," Howard said. "What are we going to offer as the prize?"

"Money," Fonzie said. "Offer the guy that wins the contest a hundred bucks. I never seen any biker yet that wouldn't risk wrecking up his thousand-dollar bike to win a hundred dollars cash."

"Where are we going to hold this contest?" Richie asked.

"Someplace soft," Howard said. "I don't want anyone to be hurt."

"Let's wait for the marshmallow highways," Potsie suggested.

"At the beach at the lake," Fonzie said. "The sand is soft enough that nobody ought to get hurt."

"Perfect," Howard said. "Let's see ... we'll need advertising—"

"That's more money going out," Richie said. "Our cash-on-hand account is about broke as it is."

"Take it out of Miscellaneous," Fonzie said.

"—newspaper ads and another television commercial," Howard went on. "And maybe we ought to use a sky writer."

"He better use red ink," Richie said.

"Got a lot to do!" Howard said, edging away. "Ads ... posters ... sky writer ... This trick riding contest is going to put the Biketeria on the map! To work! To work!" he ordered, departing. "Rebuild those bikes!"

"I am getting a little worried about your old man," Fonize said to Richie, when Howard had gone. "He's not like that at his hardware store—go, go, go, go, go—is he?"

Richie shook his head. "He enjoys the hardware store," he said.

"If he keeps this up—work, work, work—I'm going to have heartburn on my heartburn," Fonzie said. He shrugged. "I'll see you tonight," he said to Magda. "In the meantime, think about your legs, which is right and which is left. I'll be doing the same ... thinking about your legs."

"And I'll be thinking about you thinking," Magda purred.

"Hey! That is cool!"

Magda departed.

"What was so cool about her saying she'd be thinking about you thinking?" Ralph asked Fonzie.

"It wasn't her *saying* that she'd be thinking about me thinking that was cool," Fonzie replied, leading the way back into the Biketeria. "It was what she was *thinking* when she was saying she'd be thinking about me thinking."

"Oh . . ." Ralph replied. He looked puzzled at Richie and Potsie.

"I'm still trying to figure out what's cool about a piece of liver," Potsie told him.

Several days later, at dinner, Howard Cunningham announced that preparations for the trick riding contest were completed.

"The ad campaign will break tomorrow," he said. "I hired a professional announcer and a singing group to do the TV commercial. And the posters—"

"Singers, Howard?" Marion said. "What for?"

"While the announcer is making the announcement, the singers will be singing our jingle in the background," he explained. "The jingle is unforgettable.

That way, when a biker wants to buy a used bike, he'll remember our jingle and come to us."

"Who told you the jingle was unforgettable?" Fonzie asked.

"Lance Hospice. He wrote it."

"I was trying to forget him," Fonzie said.

"How does the jingle go, Dad?" Richie asked.

Howard recited. "When you want a bike that's jazzy / Come to the Bika-bika-bika-teria! / When you want a bike that's snazzy / Come to the Bika-bika-bika-teria! / Each bike we sell is a guaranteed doozy / Even though it's slightly usey! / So, come, come, come to the Bike-bike-bike-biketeria!"

"Even though it's slightly usey?" Joanie said.

"Well, we weren't entirely satisfied with that line," Howard admitted. "But Lance had to leave. He had a cocktail date with an important client."

"Excuse me," Fonzie said, getting up and leaving the table.

"He's losing another dinner," Richie said, when Fonzie had gone.

"I think it's a catchy jingle," Howard said defensively.

"I do too, dear," Marion said.

"It sure is unforgettable," Richie said.

"It certainly is," Marion said. "How does it go again, dear?" she asked Howard. "I forget."

"When you want a bike that's jazzy—"

"Hey! Will you lay off in there!" Fonzie called in from the hall. "I'm on my way back!"

"Anyway, the important thing is, the promotion campaign is ready to roll," Howard said, as Fonzie returned. "The TV commercial is set. The posters are printed. The sky writer will be overhead tomorrow at noon!"

"I'll have to remember to look up along around lunch time," Marion said.

"Friendly Foster might as well go out of business right now," Howard said. "Six months from now, we'll be the only used bike shop in town."

"That's terrible!" Marion said.

"What's terrible about it?" Howard asked.

"Well, these days, every minute that you're not asleep, you spend working on this new business," Marion replied. "If it gets any worse, you'll be thinking about it even when you're asleep. You'll be snoring that jingle."

"Mom is right, Dad," Richie said. "When was the last time you just sat down and relaxed after dinner?"

"The only time you watch television any more," Joanie said, "is when that Biketeria commercial is on."

"Maybe I am racing the old motor a little too fast . . ." Howard admitted. "All right . . . tonight, I'll relax. I'll go into the living room and sit down and watch TV . . . the whole evening . . ." He turned to Fonzie. "It wouldn't hurt you to take the night off, either, partner," he said. "You work all day, you're out all night. That's not good for you."

"Yeah, I got to cut down on that day work," Fonzie said. "Having two jobs is wearing me out."

"Two— You mean you have a night job, too?" Howard said.

"Yeah, I'm giving bike riding instructions to Magda."

Howard smiled. "Nice work."

"It's a funny thing about that job," Fonzie said. "She is the coolest female I have ever met. Right in the middle of a conversation, she will say something cool like 'London, England,' or 'the bull fights,' or 'the Eiffel tower.' But when it comes to learning to ride a bike, she will be a grandmother before she ever gets the hang of it."

"It sounds as if you're having some interesting evenings, discussing London, England and the Eiffel tower," Marion said.

"Yeah, well, that all depends on what the situation is when somebody brings up a subject like the Eiffel tower," Fonzie said.

"How far has she got, so far, learning to ride the bike, Fonz?" Richie asked.

"You remember that first day, the trouble she was having, she didn't know her left leg from her right leg? Well, we have now progressed to the point where I don't know her left leg from her right leg either." He rose. "But, no complaints," he said. "What she don't know don't hurt me." He saluted. "I will see you all around dawn, if you happen to be still up at that time," he said, leaving.

"I'm sure I won't still be awake at dawn," Howard said, getting up and heading toward the living room. "My schedule for this evening calls for sitting down in front of the television set at eight o'clock and falling asleep at eight-oh-five."

"Dad, can we talk about what those posters and that sky writer are costing?" Richie said, trailing after him. "How can I keep the books if I never get figures?"

"I haven't got the bills yet," Howard replied.

"Can't you give me an idea?" Richie asked, as they entered the living room.

"Richie, you don't put estimates in the books. When

the bills come, you pay them and record the amounts." He switched on the television set. "Let's not talk business," he said. "I'm supposed to be relaxing this evening." He sat down in his favorite chair. "Better yet, let's not talk at all. Let's just watch."

An automobile commercial came on.

"It has a strange-looking front end on it, doesn't it?" Howard said.

"I can't answer that without talking," Richie replied.

"When I said 'let's not talk,' I didn't mean that we can't say anything. I just meant, let's not get into any long-winded discussions."

"Yes," Richie said.

Howard peered at him. "Yes what?"

"Yes, it has a funny-looking front end."

Howard faced the television set again.

A Friendly Foster commercial came on. "This is it, bikers—the news you've been waiting for!" Friendly Foster announced.

"He's probably going to tell us that the fenders fall off his bikes," Howard said.

On the screen, Friendly Foster held up a poster, then read from it. "The Big Friendly Foster Trick Riding Contest!"

Howard leaped up. "What!"

"You'll be seeing these posters all over town tomorrow," Friendly Foster went on. "But, if you miss the posters, you'll see my sky writer! He'll be up bright and early in the morning! Look up and learn! Learn the details of the Giant Friendly Foster Trick Riding Contest!"

"It started out 'Big.'" Howard complained. "Now it's 'Giant!'"

"This mammoth contest will be held at the lake!" Friendly Foster continued. "And the first prize— Now, hear this, you lucky bikers! The first prize will be a gigantic, stupendous two-hundred dollars!"

Howard sank back into his chair.

"Remember, rely on the world's biggest and world's best trick riding contest—and that's Friendly Foster's! Don't accept any substitutes!"

A dog food commercial came on.

Howard groaned.

Marion and Joanie came into the room.

"We heard the commercial for your contest all the way out in the kitchen," Marion said to Howard. "But why did you have Friendly Foster do it?"

Howard moaned. "Tell her," he said to Richie.

"I don't think I can, Dad, without getting long-winded."

"Talk!" Howard commanded.

Richie explained to his mother and sister that the commercial they had heard had been Friendly Foster's, not the Biketeria's.

"Two contests?" Marion said, perplexed. "At the same place?" She brightened. "Oh, I see—a double feature!"

"There won't be two contests, Marion," Howard said drearily. "There will only be one—Friendly Foster's. If we announced our contest now, everybody would say we were copying him. I'll have to cancel our contest."

"How could they accuse you of copying him?" Joanie asked. "You had the idea first, didn't you?"

"I thought so," Howard replied. "But evidently—" He suddenly sat up straight. "We've been had!" he said. "We *did* think of it first. But Friendly Foster heard about it. He copied us—but he beat us to it!"

"That isn't a very friendly thing for a man named Friendly to do," Marion said.

"This is war, Marion," Howard said grimly.

"I wonder how he found out about our contest?" Richie said to his father.

"Well, if it's war," Marion said, "he must have found out from a spy."

Howard shook his head. "It's my fault," he said. Loose lips sink ships. I'm the blabbermouth. I was proud of that contest idea. I told a lot of people about it. And the printer who printed the posters knew about it . . . and the sky writer . . . and Lance Hospice at the advertising agency . . . Obviously, Friendly Foster heard about it and jumped right in and took it away from us."

There was a knock at the door and Richie went to answer it.

"The next idea I have, I'm going to keep it a secret," Howard said.

"Yes, order the posters, but don't tell the printer what you want printed on them," Marion said.

Answering the knock, Richie found Potsie and Ralph at the door.

"Hi!" Potsie said cheerily. "Have you watched any television lately?"

"We just turned the set off," Richie replied.

"When you had it on, did you see any commercials?" Ralph asked. "A commercial, for instance, for a car with a funny-looking front end?"

Richie nodded. "And the commercial that followed it," he said.

"Oh, boy! Then you know!" Ralph lowered his voice. "Does your father know?"

"Everybody knows," Richie replied.

"I told you we should have brought flowers," Potsie said to Ralph. He faced Richie again. "How sick is your father?" he asked.

Richie motioned. "Come on in and see for yourself."

In the living room, Howard was pacing back and forth in front of the television set when Richie and Potsie and Ralph entered. "We've got to fight fire with fire," he was saying to Marion and Joanie. "He burned us, now we've got to burn him."

"He sounds well to me," Ralph said. "He wants to set fire to Friendly Foster."

"I'm talking about taking the crowd away from Friendly Foster's trick riding contest," Howard said.

"Kidnapping?" Potsie asked.

"No, not a kidnapping!" Howard said. "Something bigger—*a lot bigger*—than a trick motorcycle riding contest!"

"How about a trick bus riding contest," Ralph suggested.

Howard stared at him.

"A bus is a lot bigger than a motorcycle," Ralph said.

"I'm not talking about a bigger vehicle, I'm talking about a bigger event!" Howard said. "Something bigger than big! Something bigger than giant! Something bigger than gigantic! Something spectacular!"

"How about shooting somebody to the moon?" Ralph said, suddenly excited. "I read the other day that someday they're going to do it. Why wait? This is a great opportunity, when we need something spectacular!"

"How do we do it?" Richie asked.

Ralph shrugged. "I don't know. The magazine I read about it in didn't say."

"Forget it," Howard said. "Nobody is ever going to go to the moon. Besides, we have to do this here in town. If we did it on the moon, who would know about it."

"It ought to be done at the lake," Richie said. "That's where Friendly Foster's crowd will be."

"Yes," Marion said. "If you're going to take the crowd away from him, you ought to make it easy on the crowd. Don't make them walk a long distance. And especially on that sandy beach. And if the ladies are wearing high heels—"

"I've got it!" Ralph said suddenly. "How about having Fonzie ride his bike along the lake!"

"What's so spectacular about that?" Howard asked.

"The *bottom* of the lake?" Ralph replied.

"Wouldn't he drown?" Joanie asked.

"You wanted spectacular," Ralph said. "You didn't say you wanted successful, too." ·

"Hey . . . what Fonzie might do . . ." Richie said. "He might jump his bike *across* the lake. The crowd would come to see that. Even the guys in the trick riding contest would probably come to see that."

"The wide end of the lake or the narrow end of the lake?" Potsie asked.

"The narrow end, of course," Richie replied. "Nobody could jump a bike across the wide end—not even The Fonz."

"I like it!" Howard said.

"It's a lot bigger than a trick riding contest," Potsie said.

"But wouldn't it be dangerous?" Marion said.

"No, nobody'll get hit by the bike," Ralph said. "We'll make sure nobody is standing on the other side."

No, won't it be dangerous for Arthur, I mean," Marion said.

"Nothing scares The Fonz," Richie said.

"But won't it be dangerous?"

"Marion, Fonzie enjoys doing spectacular things," Howard said. "He's The Fonz, remember."

"But won't it be dangerous?"

"Come on, boys," Howard said, heading for the kitchen. "We've got plans to make. Advertising ... posters ... a sky writer ..."

As they trooped out of the living room, Marion sighed resignedly. "Well, I suppose it couldn't be any more dangerous than staying up till dawn with a girl who knows about such things as the Eiffel tower and bull fighting," she said to Joanie.

FIVE

When Richie, Potsie, and Ralph arrived at the Biketeria the next morning, they found Fonzie and Magda outside. Magda was seated on Fonzie's bike. Fonzie was viewing the scene with a kind of unbelieving fascination, amazed by his success, at last, in getting Magda aboard the motorcycle.

"How did you do it, Fonz?" Richie asked.

"From sheer desperation," Fonzie replied, "I finally let my brains go all-out. I drew a picture for her."

Potsie picked up a sheet of paper from the sidewalk. "Is this it?" he asked.

"That's it—that's the picture I drew."

"But, Fonz," Potsie said, "this picture shows somebody getting *off* a bike."

"Right—I told you I let my brains go all-out. I figured, judging from all the weeks of failure, no matter what kind of picture I drew, she was gonna get it wrong. So, I drew a picture of what I didn't want her to do. And she came through with flying colors. She looked at that picture of somebody getting off a bike, she studied it, then she followed it to the letter—in that way she has—and she got *on* the bike."

78

"That's great, Fonz," Richie said. "Now, can we talk to you about something?"

"In a minute," Fonzie replied. "I got her to do something right, I don't want to lose the momentum."

"This is kind of important, Fonz, what I want to talk to you about," Richie said. "Last night—"

"Will you hold it, Cunningham?" Fonzie faced Magda. "Now, step number two," he said. "You will notice if you look around that you are sitting on the bike. So, you ask yourself what is the reason for this? Are you there to rest? No? Are you there to watch a ball game, is the bike a box seat at the ball park? No? Then the reason must be that you are on the bike to go for a ride, like you see guys doing in motorcycle movies."

"Fonz, you're so droll," Magda said sultrily.

"Droll!" Fonzie said. "Is that cool?" he asked Richie, Ralph and Potsie. "Did you hear that? Droll! Cool! What is droll?" he asked.

"Sort of funny, amusing," Richie told him.

"I knew it was good, the way it was said," Fonzie responded. "Okay," he said to Magda, "now when you're in a motorcycle movie and you see guys riding motorcycles, you notice that there is a lot of noise going on. That noise is not coming from the guy sitting next to you who is opening his box of crackerjacks. Where it is coming from is from the motors of the motorcycles. And what do we learn from that?"

Ralph spoke up. "Motorcycle motors are louder than crackerjack boxes!" they said quickly.

"Butt out, mouth."

"Sorry, Fonz. When I know the answer," Ralph said, "I can't hold back."

"That is not the answer. You get a big zero." Fonzie

faced Magda again. "What we learn from that," he informed her, "is that for a motorcycle to go, the motor has got to be running." He pointed. "Right there, that is the ignition switch that turns on the motor."

"It reminds me of the *Ponte Vecchio*," Magda said mistily.

"Cool," Fonzie said. He turned to Richie again. "What's that?"

"I don't know, Fonz."

"It's a bridge in Italy," Magda said.

Fonzie looked at the ignition switch. "That reminds you of a bridge in Italy?"

"Some mornings—mornings like this—everything reminds me of the *Ponte Vecchio*," Magda explained. "When you've seen the world, Fonz, it's inevitable that there will be times when . . ." She looked off into the distance. ". . . when your thoughts will return to one special morning on the *Ponte Vecchio* . . ."

"Yeah, well, I'll cross that bridge when I come to it," Fonzie said. "Right now, let's pay attention to the motor."

"Oh, I've been listening," Magda assured him. "I've heard everything you said." She grasped the gear shift. "This is the ignition switch," she said.

Fonzie drooped. "Well, back to the old drawing pencil," he said. "What we need here is a map, where the ignition switch is the gear shift and the accelerator is, the rear-view mirror . . ."

"Can we talk to you now, Fonz?" Richie asked.

"Yeah. I need the rest." To Magda, he said, "Take a couple minutes and concentrate on remembering where you think all the controls are. That way, when you got it in your head all wrong and you look at the map I'm gonna draw you, you'll get it right—maybe." He turned back to Richie. "Talk."

"Friendly Foster stole our idea for a trick riding contest," Richie told him.

"I kind of figured that out when I saw that sky writer this morning," Fonzie said. "There he was, up above the earth so high, advertising our contest, only he was spelling Biketeria F-r-i-e-n-d-l-y "F-o-s-t-e-r.'" He pointed toward the shop. "Also, we have a Friendly Foster trick riding contest poster in the window."

"Aren't you mad?" Ralph asked.

"Sure, I'm mad," Fonzie replied. "The next time I go by that window, I'm gonna take that poster out."

"Anyway," Richie said, "we're going to fight fire with fire."

"You mean—"

"No," Ralph said. "That's what I thought, too. But it turns out, there's a law against setting Friendly Foster on fire."

"What we're going to do," Potsie told Fonzie, "is stage an event that will take the crowd away from Friendly Foster's contest."

"Now, that is smart thinking," Fonzie said.

"We're going to have you jump your bike over the lake," Richie said.

"Now, that is dumb thinking," Fonzie said.

"The narrow end," Ralph told him. "We wouldn't ask you to jump your bike over the wide end. Nobody could do that, not even The Fonz."

"Nobody could jump a bike over the narrow end, either," Fonzie said. "The farthest a bike could be jumped would be about halfway. The rest of the jump would be swimming."

"Come on, Fonz, you can do it," Potsie said.

"How many times have you jumped a bike over anything?" Fonzie asked him.

"All told?"

"Counting every single time."

"None."

"Then who knows better how far a bike can be jumped?" Fonzie asked.

"Fonz," Richie said, "the Biketeria really needs this. We're at war with Friendly Foster."

"What if we lose?" Fonzie asked.

"We'll probably lose the business," Richie replied.

"Yeah, and even if you don't jump the narrow end of the lake," Ralph told Fonzie, "the worst that can happen is that you'll get a little wet."

"Then, you do the jumping," Fonzie replied.

"I catch cold when I get wet," Ralph said.

"What do you think I catch—hot?"

"But, you might make it," Potsie argued. "It's just possible, Fonz. If anybody can jump the narrow end of the lake, you can. If we were asking you to jump the *wide* end of the lake, that would be different. But the narrow end ... who knows, a miracle might happen."

"A wind might come along and carry you over," Ralph said.

"A tornado!" Potsie said. "Just when you jump, we might have a tornado. You could be caught up in it and be carried clear across the lake!"

"Or the government might build a marshmallow road under me just when I jump," Fonzie said.

"I think that's expecting a little too much, Fonz," Potsie said.

"At least think about it before you definitely say no, Fonz," Richie said.

"Okay, I will think about it." Fonzie frowned deeply. "I thought about it," he announced. "I will not try to jump the narrow end of the lake."

Richie, Potsie, and Ralph groaned as one.

"What I will do is, I will jump the wide end of the lake," Fonzie said.

"That's not droll, Fonz," Richie said.

"Who is drolling? I'm telling you, I will jump the wide end of the lake."

"How?" Richie asked skeptically.

"That is for me to know and you to find out when I do it," Fonzie replied. "I am not telling anybody how. If I do, Friendly Foster will find out how and will get some other nerd to do it first, like he stole the idea for the trick riding contest."

"No, Fonz, you can't do it," Richie said. "It would be too dangerous. To jump the wide end of the lake, you'd need a takeoff ramp that would shoot you really high. I mean *really* high. If you fell from that distance, you could—" He shook his head. "You can't do it. It's too dangerous."

"Yeah, getting wet and catching cold can be cured," Potsie said to Fonzie. "But what could happen to you if you tried to jump the wide end of the lake could be permanent."

"I made up my mind," Fonzie said. "When somebody said nobody could jump the wide end of the lake, not even The Fonz, that's what did it. What nobody can do—not even The Fonz—The Fonz can do!" He returned his attention to Magda. "Okay, you got the controls straight in your head?" he asked. "Where is the ignition?"

She pointed to the gear shift.

"Right," he said. "Now, where is the gears?"

She pointed to the ignition.

"You got it," Fonzie told her. "All you got to remember now is, to start the motor, you switch on the gear shift. Try it."

Magda started the engine.

"He's really teaching her," Ralph said. "If he can do that, maybe he really *can* jump the wide end of the lake."

A few nights later, the Cunninghams gathered around the TV set to watch the opening commercial for Fonzie's planned attempt to jump the wide end of the lake on his bike. From upstairs came the sound of hammering.

"What is Fonzie doing up there in his room?" Howard complained. "How are we going to hear the commercial with all that racket going on?"

"He must be building something," Marion said. "Maybe he's putting in book shelves."

"Did someone give him a book?" Joanie asked.

"I don't think it's book shelves," Richie said. "It sounds like he's pounding on metal."

"Iron book shelves," Marion guessed. "He probably wants them to last."

"Shhh! Here comes the commercial!" Howard said.

A professional announcer appeared on the screen. Behind him was a singing group.

"Big! Gigantic! Stupendous!" the announcer announced.

"Lance Hospice wrote that," Howard said. "He has a way with words.

Behind the announcer, the singing group began singing the Biketeria jingle—softly. "When you want a bike that's snazzy . . . When you want a bike that's jazzy . . ."

"The feat of the century!" the announcer boomed. "See it live! A motorcycle extravaganza! The Fonz leaps the wide end of the lake!"

The singing group came in again. "Each bike we sell is a guaranteed doozy . . . Even though it's slightly usey . . ."

The announcer took over once more. "Death-defying! Be there when The Fonz soars to unprecedented heights! Be there at the finish!"

"I don't like the way he said that," Marion said. "He sounded like he meant Arthur's finish."

"That's what makes him a professional announcer," Howard explained. "He has the voice of doom."

The commercial ended with the final line of the jingle. ". . . come, come, come to the Bike-bike-bike-biketeria!"

Howard turned off the set. "I'll bet Friendly Foster is looking for a way to commit suicide right now," he said happily.

Fonzie appeared. "Hey," he said to Marion, "have you got a sheet you could lend me the borrow of?"

"A sheet, Arthur?"

"Yeah, one of those things you put two of them on the bed, only I only need one."

"Why, yes . . ." Marion said.

"Fonzie, are you building an iron bed?" Howard asked.

"An iron bed? What would I want with an iron bed? If I turned over in my sleep and banged my head on it, I could knock myself cuckoo."

"Then what is that pounding?" Howard asked.

"That's a secret bike," Fonzie replied.

"A secret—"

"I can't jump the wide end of the lake on no ordinary bike," Fonzie said. "So, I'm building a secret bike."

"Out of a sheet?"

"Don't ask me no details," Fonzie said. "Nobody sees this bike until I'm ready to make my jump. I'm not taking any chances on Friendly Foster finding out how the bike is built and making up a secret bike himself."

Marion, who had gone after a sheet, returned with it. "It's freshly washed," she said, handing it to Fonzie. "I hope you'll be comfy."

"It's for a bike," Fonzie told her.

"Oh. Well, then, I hope the bike will be comfy."

Fonzie departed, returning to his room.

"I hope he knows what he's doing," Howard said. "I don't see how a sheet is going to get him across the wide end of the lake."

"Maybe it's a net, to catch him when he gets there," Joanie said.

"Possible ... but a sheet won't make a very strong net ..."

There was a knock at the door.

"Potsie and Ralph," Richie said, going to answer it. But when he opened the door he found Magda there. "Hi!" he said. "Are you looking for Fonzie'"

"Is he lost?" Magda asked, slinking into the house.

"He's up in his room," Richie replied, closing the door.

"We were to have a tete-a-tete," Magda said. "But he didn't appear. That's why I thought he might be lost."

"Boy!" Richie said. "A tete-a-tete!"

The sound of pounding was heard again.

"Ok, does Fonzie bring his work home with him?" Magda asked.

"No," Howard said, "he's building a bike to jump the wide end of the lake with. Richie," he said, "go up to Fonzie's room and tell him that Magda is here."

"Yes," Magda said, as Richie left, "he was supposed to give me another lesson in night riding."

"Won't you sit down?" Marion said. "We can have a little talk while we're waiting."

"Well . . . I don't speak Milwaukee very well . . ." Magda said, setting in a chair.

"That's all right," Marion said. "I think I still remember some of my high school sophisticated. Ahhhh . . . Piccadilly Circus," she said.

Magda smiled amusedly. "*Champs Elysees*," she responded.

"Budapest," Marion said brightly.

Magda smiled sadly. "*Portofino*," she said.

Joanie whispered to her father. "What are they saying?" she asked.

"Nothing." Howard whispered back. "They're telling each other how sophisticated they are."

"*Ole!*" Marion said spiritedly.

"Atlantic City," Magda responded. "Oops—I'm sorry," she said immediately "*St. Tropez*, I meant."

They heard Richie returning.

"Well, nice having this little chat," Marion said to Magda.

"Likewise, I'm sure."

"Mom, I didn't know you were sophisticated," Joanie said.

"I've always been sophisticated, dear," Marion replied. "I just haven't had anyone to talk sophisticated to."

Richie reappeared. "I'm sorry," he said to Magda. "Fonzie won't come down. He wouldn't even open the door of his room. He says he can't leave his secret bike. But he sent along your night riding lesson," he said. "You're supposed to switch on the brake."

" 'Switch on' the brake?" Howard said. "Are you sure that's what he said, Richie?"

Richie nodded. "Don't worry about it, Dad. When she switches on what she thinks is the brake, the headlight will go on."

"This secret bike . . . how droll," Magda said, amused.

"Yes, it certainly is," Marion said. "It sleeps under a sheet."

"What else do you know about it?" Magda asked.

"Other than that you can't keep books on it, nothing," Marion told her. "Arthur won't tell us anything. He's afraid Friendly Foster will learn the secret."

"How droll," Magda said. "I wonder," she said to Richie, "would it be possible for me to go up to Fonzie's room and speak to him through his keyhole?"

"You could talk to him through the door," Richie replied. "You wouldn't have to talk through the keyhole. Anyway, he's hung something over the keyhole on the inside. I tried to look through it to get a peek at the secret bike. Do you want to go up and talk to him through the door?" he asked.

"No, I don't want to bruise my voice," Magda replied, purring. She turned to Marion. "I must be on my way," she said. "Ta-ta."

"*Auf wiedersehen*," Marion replied.

"*Adieu*," Magda said, moving toward the door.

"*Adios!*" Marion called after her.

"*Addio!*" Magda replied, departing.

The door closed.

"Darn!" Marion said. "I still had *aloha* to go!"

"That was marvelous, Marion," Howard said. "You did Milwaukee proud."

"There was just one word I didn't understand," Joanie said to her mother. "What is '*ole!*'?"

"Oh ... that's Spanish, dear," Marion replied. "It means, 'Oh, what a beautiful cape!'"

"Uh ... are you sure about that?" Howard asked.

"Positive, dear. I learned it from a newsreel years ago. There was a picture of all these people in the seats in a huge arena and they were all shouting '*Ole!*' And then in the next picture a young man in the middle of the arena was showing off his cape. It was a *lovely* cape."

"Then, I guess that's what it means," Howard said.

From upstairs came the sound of pounding again.

"I hope that isn't going to go on all night," Howard said. "How are we going to get any sleep?"

"Dear, be patient," Marion said. "Fonzie is doing it for you."

"He's doing it for the Biketeria," Howard said. "Don't forget, we're partners."

"But I think you're more of a partner than Fonzie is," Marion said.

"Marion, that's impossible. Partners means sharing, half and half."

"Howard, you know very well that there's a big half and a little half to everything. Marriage is a partnership, too, but you weigh more than I do."

"Weight has nothing—" He interrupted himself,

cocking an ear. "What was that?" he said. "I heard something."

"That was Fonzie, Dad," Richie said.

"No ... this was a different sound ..." He looked toward the door. "I think it came from outside."

"I'll check," Richie said, going toward the door.

"As I was saying," Howard went on, addressing Marion again, "the Biketeria is as important to Fonzie as it is to me. He wants to be the used bike king of the country as much as I do."

"I don't see Fonzie sitting around cutting out paper crowns," Marion said.

"Marion, I wasn't serious about those paper crowns. I was just doodling ... and I happened to have a pair of scissors and some gold paper in my hands. If I—" He interrupted himself again, looking toward the open doorway. "Is Richie talking to someone out there?"

"I only hear one voice," Joanie said. "He must be talking to himself."

"Or to someone who speaks very softly," Marion said.

At that moment, Richie returned.

"Was there somebody out there?" Howard asked.

Richie nodded. "Magda."

"What was she—"

"She was putting our ladder up against the house, under Fonzie's window," Richie replied.

The other stared at him baffled.

"She said she found the ladder in the yard and she didn't want anybody to fall over it, so, to get it out of the way, she was leaning it against the house," Richie explained.

"How nice!" Marion said.

"I thanked her," Richie said.

"We keep the ladder in the garage," Howard said.

"Somebody must have left it out," Richie said.

"How droll," Joanie said.

"Droll means funny," Richie told her.

"Right—it seems kind of funny to me that she would be putting the ladder right under Fonzie's window," Joanie said.

The telephone rang.

Howard picked up the receiver and identified himself, then began a conversation. "Well . . . I waltz . . . and the two-step . . ."

"It's that policeman, selling tickets to the Ball," Marion said to Joanie and Richie.

"Yes, I know, a promise is a promise," Howard said into the receiver. "What would I— What? Where? All right, twelve tickets! Yes! Right! On the highway! Twenty! All over the road?"

"Something terrible has happened out on the highway!" Marion said.

"I'm on my way!" Howard said into the phone. "Don't move anything!" He hung up.

"Is it an accident?" Marion asked. "It sounds horrible!"

"Yes, an accident!" Howard replied. "It's wonderful!"

"Wonderful? Howard, you don't mean that! How many were hurt?"

"Hurt? Marion, what are you talking about?"

"How many people were hurt?"

"Not people," Howard replied. "Motorcycles! A truck turned over out on the highway. The driver wasn't hurt. But the motorcycles were wrecked! All twenty of them! Come on," he said to Richie. "We've got to get out there and buy up those wrecked bikes before Friendly Frost gets wind of this!"

"Drive carefully, Howard!" Marion called after them. "Don't have an accident on the way to the accident!"

"This is going to cost me twelve tickets to the Policemen's Ball, but it's worth it," Howard said to Richie as they drove off a few minutes later in the family car. "I ought to be able to buy those wrecked bikes for a song!"

"Not that jingle, I hope," Richie said.

"You sound like your mother," Howard said. "Why do I have the feeling that I'm the only one in the family who wants to become the used bike king? Doesn't your mother realize that that will make her the used bike queen? And you—you'll be the used bike prince."

"I don't know ... everything's so different, that's all," Richie said. "You never wanted to be the hardware store king."

"I was a stick-in-the-mud until I discovered used bikes," Howard said. "Say!—that might make a good article for *Readers' Digest!*" he said. "That is, when they get around to carrying the condensation of my autobiography."

"You almost went through a red light," Richie said.

"Almost doesn't count. I've got to hurry. Do you want Friendly Foster to beat me to those bikes?"

"Did that officer call him, too?"

"No, but Friendly Foster monitors all police calls. He's on his way to that accident, too, you can bet on that." He leaned forward. "There's the ramp to the highway. We're almost there!" Leaning back, he looked in the rear-view mirror. "Oh-oh! Here comes Friendly Foster on his bike!" Howard stepped hard on the accelerator. "Hold on!"

Richie looked out the rear window. "Boy, he's coming fast!"

Howard swerved the car onto the ramp, tires squealing.

"You told me never to drive like this!" Richie said.

"Didn't I add—'unless you want to be the used bike king of the country?'"

"No."

"Well, I meant to," Howard said. "It slipped my mind." He swung the car onto the highway. "There's the wreck!" he said exultantly. "We're here first!"

Richie saw a large truck that was tipped over on its side. Damaged bikes were strewn along the side of the highway. Two police cars were parked near the truck.

Pulling over onto the shoulder, Howard jammed on the brakes. The car skidded, then came to a stop.

"Come on!" Howard said, jumping out of the car. "We've got to find the owner!"

Friendly Foster's bike skidded to a halt behind the Cunningham car.

"I heard about it first!" Friendly Foster shouted, leaping from the bike. "All the wrecks belong to me!"

"I *got* here first!" Howard shouted back at him. "The wrecks are mine!"

Officer McWorter appeared. "I got your twelve tickets right here," he said to Howard.

"Later!" Howard said. "Where is the owner?"

McWorter pointed. "Over there by his truck."

Howard and Friendly Foster raced off. Richie trailed after them at a much slower pace. By the time he caught up with them they had located the owner of the truck, a big, thickly-muscled man, who was chewing on the stub of an unlighted cigar. The bidding for the bikes had already started.

"Ten!" Friendly Foster said.

"Fifteen!" Howard countered.

"Twenty!" Friendly Foster said.

"Twenty-one-fifty!" Howard offered.

"Wasn't twenty-five supposed to come next?" the truck owner said.

"Yeah—cheapo!" Friendly Foster said to Howard. He faced the truck owner again. "Twenty-five!"

"Who's a cheapo!" Howard raged at Friendly Foster.

"If the shoe fits, put it on."

"Contest thief!" Howard charged.

"Contest spoiler!" Friendly Foster shot back. "You and your wide end of the lake!"

"How would you like to have a nose you could rent out as a dirigible!" Howard threatened.

"Who's gonna do it?" Friendly Foster challenged.

"Me, that's who!"

"You and who else?"

Howard responded with another threat. "When I get through with you, you'll be wearing your teeth as a necklace!"

"Hey . . ." the truck owner said calmly.

Howard and Friendly Foster ignored him.

"If I ever hit you," Foster said to Howard, "I'll knock you so far out of town, it'll cost you a month's profits to buy a railroad ticket back!"

"Hey . . ." the truck owner said, a little more strongly.

"If I ever hit you—" Howard began, addressing Friendly Foster again.

But at that moment the truck owner got the two men by the back of the neck and pulled them far apart. "Hey!" he said loudly.

Friendly Foster opened his mouth.

"Shaddup!" the truck owner said.

Friendly Foster closed his mouth.

"I got a headache from turning over my truck," the owner told them. "All that noise is giving my headache a headache. Now, you guys want to buy those wrecked bikes, it's okay with me. The price is fifty bucks a bike. There is twenty bikes. You," he said to Howard, "get ten of them. And you," he said to Friendly Foster, "get the other ten of them."

Howard opened his mouth.

"And if I hear any squawks, I bang your heads together," the truck owner said.

"Fifty dollars and ten and ten, that seems fair to me," Howard said.

"I'm a very peaceful person," Friendly Foster said. "All I wanted was a fair deal." He pointed to Howard. "He was the one who started all the—"

"Shaddup!" the truck owner said again. He released Howard and Friendly Foster. "Write me your checks. Only *quiet!*" he shouted. He grasped his head painfully. "You got me doing it," he wailed.

Howard and Richie withdrew so that Howard could write out a check for the truck owner.

"I see what you mean about this used bike business changing things," Howard said.

"Boy, I'm glad, Dad!"

"It's turned that Foster into a monster," Howard said. "I'm glad it hasn't effected me that way. Poor

Foster. But, as Harry says, if you can't stand the heat, stay out of the kitchen."

"Harry who?" Richie asked.

Howard looked at him in surprise. "That's very well known," he said. "Don't you know whose saying that is?"

Richie shook his head.

"Harry Honski," Howard told him, writing the check. "He's the cook at the diner near the hardware store."

SIX

Arriving at the Biketeria, Howard found Magda sitting outside on Fonzie's bike. She appeared to be waiting for something to happen.

"Good morning," he said.

"*Guten morgen.*"

"I'm sorry, I only speak Milwaukee," Howard said. He gestured toward the shop. "Are you going in?"

"I'm taking a lesson," she replied.

"Alone?"

"No, Fonzie—"

At that moment, Fonzie came hurrying from the shop, looking harried. He appeared to be unaware of Howard. "Make sure your headlight is in neutral, switch on your gear and accelerate your brake," he said to Magda. Then, with Magda looking after him dazedly, he hustled back into the Biketeria.

"Did he say what I thought he said?" Howard asked.

"Probably," Magda replied. She looked back at the rear tire. "Does that headlight look a little low to you?"

Not knowing how to answer that question, Howard

left her and entered the shop. Fonzie was accepting money from a red-headed young man, a customer who had just purchased a bike that Howard had bought from the truck owner and that had since been rebuilt.

"Is that right?" the young man asked Fonzie, putting the last bill into his hand.

Fonzie took a last look at the bike that he had sold to the young man. "The paint job don't knock my eyes out the way it should," he said. "You overpaid by twenty bucks," he said, handing one of the bills back to the young man.

"Wow—are you honest!"

"It's a family curse," Fonzie told him. "Honest but poor. When we die, we can't even afford a new suit for the burial, we're put away in our underwear."

As the red-headed young man wheeled the bike from the shop, Fonzie darted away, rushing to the rear of the shop, where he resumed work on rebuilding the rest of the bikes that had been purchased from the truck owner. He still seemed to be completely unaware of Howard.

"Fonzie . . . it's me . . . I'm here . . ." Howard said.

"I'll take your word for it," Fonzie replied, fitting a carburetor onto an engine. "I haven't got time to look."

"What's all this rush?"

"Figure it out," Fonzie replied. "I got bikes to rebuild, I got bikes to sell, I got my secret bike to put together, I got lessons to give to Magda, and, also with Magda, I got a little of this and a little of that. I haven't got time to do anything but rush."

"That *is* a lot to do," Howard agreed. "You ought to

give something up. How about cutting down on the this and that?"

"The this and that is the only thing that makes the rest of it bearable," Fonzie told him. "Take away the this and that and I might as well strip down to my underwear and move on out to the cemetery."

"Why isn't Richie helping?"

"He helps," Fonzie replied. "Potsie and Ralph help, too. But they don't have all the privileges of being a partner—they can sleep late and they can take off and go to a ball game if they feel like it, which is where they are now. Me, with my privileges, I got to be here and work."

The red-headed young man returned, wheeling the bike back into the shop, looking considerably less happy than when he left. "Some honest!" the young man said. "I only got as far as the corner and the motor came down with pneumonia."

"What're you talking about?" Fonzie replied. "Any motor that leaves this shop is as healthy as a horse."

The young man started the bike's motor. It coughed, wheezed, then died.

"That couldn't be the engine that left here a couple minutes ago," Fonzie said. "What're you trying to do, palm off a bum engine on us?" he said to the young man. Leaning over, he looked closely at the motor. "That's the same engine," he said.

"What happened to it?" Howard asked.

"How do I know?" Fonzie started the engine again. As before, it began wheezing and coughing. "Somebody adjusted it all out of adjustment," he said. He got tools and began working on it.

"Fonzie, we can't afford to turn out shoddy work

like that," Howard said. "Word will get out. We won't have any customers."

"It's a freak accident," Fonzie said. "Nothing like this couldn't happen again in a hundred years. When The Fonz puts an engine together, it purrs like clockwork." He stepped back. The engine was now purring. "Hear that? Tick-tock, tick-tock. It's as healthy as a horse again."

"I'll take your word for it," Howard said. "I'm not sure whether I should be listening for a cat purring, a clock ticking or a horse whinnying."

"It sounds great," the red-headed young man said to Fonzie.

"Just keep it out of drafts," Fonzie told him. "It's got a delicate constitution."

The young man wheeled the bike out. But, as he was departing, another young man wheeled a bike in.

"You sold me a clunker!" the newcomer said angrily.

"Heyyyy! Nobody says that to The Fonz! How would you like to be riding that bike from the inside out?"

The young man peered at him puzzled.

"Which is what you'll be doing after I ram it down your throat," Fonzie told him.

"Fonzie, that is no way to treat a customer," Howard said. "Find out what his problem is."

"My problem is this bike I bought here yesterday," the young man said to Howard. "Today, the front wheel is coming off." He shook the bike. "See?"

"That is a loose front wheel," Fonzie agreed. He reached for his tools. "There must be a pneumonia and loose wheel germ going around," he said. "When

I finished putting that bike together, that front wheel was as tight as a bum."

"Tight as a drum," the young man said.

"Tight as a bum," Fonzie replied, working on the wheel. "This bum I'm talking about is a wino." He stepped back. "It's A—1 again," he told the young man. "And I accept your apology for that crack you made about a 'clunker' when you first came in. The Fonz guarantees his work."

"What if I have more trouble?" the young man asked.

"See a doctor about yourself," Fonzie replied. "I don't guarantee the customers."

The young man wheeled the bike out.

"Fonzie, you're trying to do too much," Howard said. "You're turning out shoddy merchandise."

"Never," Fonzie replied. "The lessons I'm giving Magda, I admit, are not the best—and the this and that is not up to the usual Fonz standards, either. And maybe I fall a little short as a bike salesman. But when I rebuild a bike, it's the best job that can be done."

"Then how do you explain what's happening, all these bikes being brought back?" Howard asked. "Is it because Richie and Potsie and Ralph are helping you with the rebuilding? Are they making the mistakes?"

Fonzie shook his head. "I inspect everything they do," he said. "When a bike goes on sale, it's got the Fonz's one-hundred proof okay. What is happening to those bikes is happening *after* they get The Fonz's nod."

"I don't understand."

"We got a sabotager in the ointment," Fonzie told him.

"You mean someone is damaging the bikes after you okay them? Who?"

"It's got to be me or Richie or Potsie or Ralph," Fonzie replied. "Nobody else gets near those bikes. Except Magda," he added, "and she is eliminated by the process of not knowing a headlight from a back tire."

Magda entered. "I'm afraid your bike is terribly ill," she said to Fonzie. "The motor went 'burp-burp-burp,' then it stopped completely."

"Burp, burp, burp, that's gas," Fonzie said.

"Fonzie, I am willing to believe a lot of things, but I will not believe that a motorcycle gets gas," Howard said.

"Not gets gas, it's out of gas," Fonzie told him. "That's why it stopped." He turned to Magda again. "All the time you been hanging around here, have you seen anybody suspicious?" he asked. "Somebody is sabotaging our bikes.

"I've never trusted that one with freckles," Magda said.

Howard shook his head. "No, Ralph is completely trustworthy," he said. "Ralph has been my son's friend for—" He suddenly looked thoughtful. "But, then, why did he become Richie's friend? Has he been planning this all these years, waiting for this opportunity?"

"It's not Ralph," Fonzie said. "I would trust Ralph with Potsie's life."

"Well ... maybe it isn't sabotage after all," Howard said. "Mistakes happen. Maybe just this once—twice, actually—you booted it," he said to Fonzie. "You're only human, you know."

"Bite your tongue!" Fonzie said indignantly.

"Not to change the subject, I think I'll change the subject," Howard said. "What I came over here for was to find out what you think about a price-cutting campaign. These bikes you're rebuilding aren't moving fast enough."

"That's not the prices, that sounds like carburetor trouble to me," Fonzie said.

"I mean they're not selling fast enough."

"What's the hurry?" Fonzie asked. "You know what we're going to have when we sell all these bikes, don't you? We're gonna have an empty store. That means we got to get out and get more wrecks. It gets to be a vicious circle. I say, let's leave well enough alone."

"Fonzie, that's turnover, that's what business is," Howard said. "That's how we're going to make money, that's how we're going to open branches, that's how we're going to become the used bike kings."

"Instead of kings," Fonzie replied, "how about we settle for prime minister and close up the shop and go out and see the ball game with Richie?"

"Kings or nothing," Howard insisted. "What do you think of the price-cutting idea?"

"If we cut the prices, where is the profit?"

"We won't cut the prices *that* much," Howard replied. "We'll only cut them enough so that we'll be under-selling Friendly Foster. That way, we'll get all the business. Or, at least, the lion's share of it." He turned to Magda. "How does it sound to you, as a prospective motorcycle buyer?" he asked.

"Simba," she replied.

"Pardon?"

"I think that's Swahili for 'lion,'" she replied. "That or it was the name of my hairdresser in Mozambique."

"Cool!" Fonzie said. "Mozambique!

"Yes ..." Howard said. "But doesn't anybody have a comment on the price-cutting idea?"

"How much below what Friendly Foster charges are we going to cut our prices?" Fonzie asked.

"Five percent was the figure I had in mind."

"Make it six," Fonzie said.

"Six?" Howard pondered for a second. "What's your thinking on that?" he asked Fonzie.

"The number five has got that sharp corner at the top," Fonzie replied, "but the number six is smooth all the way around. I like a smooth number."

"Thank you," Magda purred. "I just adore you, too, Fonzie, dear."

Howard made a face of dismay. "This is serious," he said. "I think a five percent cut is as far as we can go. Since our profit margin is ten percent, that will reduce it to five percent. If we go any lower, we'll be in trouble. Because, of course, as soon as we announce our price cut, Friendly Foster will retaliate with a price cut of his own. And that means that, to compete, we'll have to cut our prices still more. With only five percent to work with, we'll be walking a very fine line."

"Simba," Magda said.

"Line, not 'lion,'" Howard told her.

"Yeah, you go walking a lion around in Milwaukee and you'll find yourself in the clink," Fonzie said. "Milwaukee is no Mozambique."

Richie, Potsie, and Ralph entered.

"Who won the game?" Fonzie asked.

"We don't know," Richie replied. "We left at the end of the second inning."

"What'd you do that for?"

"The score was twenty-five to nothing," Potsie explained.

"But you don't know who won?"

"Well, with seven innings to go, our team could still pull it out," Richie said. "All it would take would be for every batter to hit a grand-slam homer. What are the chances of that happening, though?"

"Maybe five-and-a-half percent," Howard said, talking to mself.

"More like a million-to-one," Ralph said.

"I'm thinking about cutting prices," Howard said to Richie. "What do you think?"

"Dad, I don't get enough allowance as it is," Richie protested.

"Not the price of keeping you in hamburgers, the prices here at the Biketeria," Howard said. "I'm thinking about a five percent reduction. That would force Friendly Foster, when he retaliates, to go to a seven or eight percent cut to get any attention."

"So?" Fonzie said.

"Then we go to ten percent," Howard replied.

"We'll only be breaking even," Fonzie pointed out.

"Yes! But when Friendly Foster makes his next cut, he'll have to go *below* ten percent. If he's working on the same profit margin we are, he'll then be selling his bikes at a loss! How long can he keep that up? A week, two weeks, a month at the most, and he'll be bankrupt!"

"You got the heart of a nerd," Fonzie told Howard.

"It's just business," Howard said. "If we didn't do it to him, he'd do it to us. Get ready for the rush," he said, heading for the door. "As soon as I figure out exactly how much to cut prices and make the announcement on television, we'll be overrun with buyers."

"Okay, you heard him," Fonzie said to Richie, Potsie, and Ralph. "Vacation is over. We got to get busy rebuilding these bikes. What I want you to do," he said, "is get together all the parts that you see lyin' around."

Magda corrected him. "Simba around," he said.

"Cool!" Fonzie said in wonder. He began directing the collecting of the parts. "You guys don't know what you missed going to that ballgame," he said. "While you was gone, she said . . . She said . . . Mozambique . . . Heyyyyyyyy!"

After dinner that evening, Howard settled in his favorite chair in the living room with several pads of paper and a number of freshly-sharpened pencils. As he began figuring, however, the sound of pounding came from upstairs. Howard glared in the direction of the second floor, then, grimacing, stuck a finger in an ear and tried to resume the figuring. The pounding grew louder. After a few more minutes, Howard gave up the figuring and stuck both fingers in his ears. That was how Richie found him.

"Is that yoga?" Richie asked.

Howard removed one finger from one ear. "What?"

"I asked if that's yoga."

"What is yoga?"

"It's a new thing some of the kids are doing," Richie replied. "You sit around with your legs crossed and meditate."

"Are my legs crossed?"

"Well . . . at your age, I thought maybe you

couldn't cross your legs any more," Richie replied, "so you stuck your fingers in your ears."

"I stuck my fingers in my ears to keep out the noise," Howard told him. "I can't concentrate with that pounding gong on."

"Why don't you do what I do?" Richie said. "When I'm trying to study and there's a lot of noise around, I turn on the TV and turn up the sound loud, then I can't hear the noise."

"Richie—" Howard considered for a moment. "I suppose it might work," he said. He got up and switched on the television set, then returned to his chair. A second later, a news program came on, with the sound booming from the set. Quickly, Howard stuck his fingers back in his ears.

"You have to get used to it!" Richie said.

"What?"

"Get used to it!" Richie shouted.

Slowly, Howard began removing his fingers from his ears. "I see what you mean," he shouted back to Richie. "It really works! I can't hear that pounding any more!"

Fonzie appeared.

"That's why you can't hear the pounding!" Richie shouted to his father. "He *stopped* pounding!"

"Hey, you got a pipe?" Fonzie asked Howard.

"I don't smoke a pipe!"

"Okay, okay, you don't have to shout. I don't mean that kind of pipe, anyway. I'm talking about the kind of pipe that when the plumber comes to fix the sink he hasn't got the right size of and has to go back to the shop and get it."

"Look in the basement!" Howard suggested, shouting.

Fonzie went to the television set and lowered the volume. "Hasn't anybody but me got any brains around here?" he said. "That's all you got to do—turn the sound down. Then you don't have to shout," he said, departing.

Howard resumed the figuring.

"What're all those numbers for?" Richie asked.

"I'm plotting price reductions, ours and Friendly Fosters," Howard replied. "The calculations have to be perfect. Otherwise, we'll be the ones who end up selling bikes at a loss. What it depends on, the way I figure, is who gets the jump on who."

"Who starts the price cuts, you mean?"

"Right. As I explained this afternoon, we go to five, he goes to seven-or-eight, then we go to ten, then he has nowhere to go but bankruptcy. That's why, tomorrow morning, first thing, I'm going down to the TV station and arrange for our price-cut commercial. I want to have it on the air by tomorrow night."

The sound of pounding came from upstairs again.

Howard stuck his fingers back into his ears.

Richie turned up the volume on the TV set.

Howard removed his fingers from his ears.

A Friendly Foster commercial came on.

"It's the news you been waiting for, bikers!" Friendly Foster boomed from the television screen. "The Big Giant Friendly Foster Summer Sale on used bikes! Prices slashed by five percent on every used bike in stock! Just like I said last summer—there'll never be another sale like it! It's so big and giant, it's colossal!"

"I think he has Lance Hospice writing for him," Richie said.

"Stop him!" Howard shouted. "He can't do this!"

"Prices cut by five percent!" Friendly Foster roared from the TV set. "You can't beat that anywhere else in town. Friendly Foster's Gigantic Summer Sale features the itty-bittiest prices in Milwaukee! Stock up now! Buy bikes for the whole family!"

Howard rushed at the set and turned it off. "Thief!" he shouted at the silent set. "You stole my price reductions!"

"Dad, take it easy!"

"I'll retaliate!" Howard shouted. "I'll cut prices at the Biketeria by eight percent!"

"And he'll go to ten," Richie said.

"And I'll go bankrupt!" Howard bellowed.

Marion came hurrying into the room. "Howard! Will you stop that shouting! I can't hear Arthur's pounding!"

"You can't—" Howard stared at her dumbly. "Marion, that doesn't make any sense."

"It makes as much sense as shouting at a television set that isn't even turned on," she countered.

"She's right, Dad," Richie said. "Forget it. Friendly Foster got the jump on you and that's that."

Howard sank into his chair. "How did he do it? I understand how he found out about the trick riding contest. But how did he find out about the price cuts? I haven't told anyone."

"Probably just coincidence," Richie said.

Howard shook his head. "No . . ." He raised his eyes to Richie. "Did we have any more dissatisfied customers after I left the Biketeria today?" he asked.

"Guys bringing their bikes back? Yeah. Three more."

"Fonzie is right," Howard said. "We have a saboteur in our midst. And that saboteur is also a spy!"

"Don't you have insurance for that, Howard?" Marion asked.

"For somebody who's a saboteur and a spy? What kind of insurance?"

"Double identity."

"That's double indemnity, Marion, and it doesn't apply to this situation." He frowned deeply. "Who is it? Potsie or Ralph?"

"Hey, Dad!" Richie protested. "It's not Potsie or Ralph!"

"Then, it's you," Howard told him. "You're the only other logical suspect. Who had the opportunity to sabotage those bikes? You and Potsie and Ralph. Who knew about my plan to cut prices? You and Potsie and Ralph."

"And Magda," Richie said. "She's always hanging around."

"Richie, honestly, do you believe that Magda could sabotage a carburetor?" Howard asked. "She wouldn't even know where to look for a carburetor."

"Well . . . But she could have told Friendly Foster about the plan for the price cut."

"Why would she? Besides, he wouldn't understand her even if she did tell him. I'm sure Friendly Foster doesn't speak Swahili."

"I guess she's not the most likely suspect," Richie conceded. "But Potsie or Ralph didn't do it, either."

"We'll find out when we get the report from the private detective, Howard said

"Dad, you can't do that!"

"You certainly can't, Howard, Marion said. "When you start putting a private detective on the trail of your best friends, it's time to call a halt to—"

Howard interrupted. "Marion, Potsie and Ralph

aren't my best friends. They're not my friends at all. They're Richie's friends. Let's let the private detective decide which one is guilty, Potsie or Ralph or Richie.

"Howard!" Marion said, aghast. "Your own son? You'd hire a private detective to—"

Howard raised his hands in a sign of surrender. "Don't say it, Marion. You're right, that was a terrible thing for me to even consider. Richie," he said, "I apologize."

"That's okay, Dad."

Fonzie's pounding had stopped for a while, but now it began again.

"That's all we have left," Howard said. "Friendly Foster and his spy have won the battle of the trick riding contest and the battle of the prices. If we lose the battle of the wide end of the lake . . . the war is lost . . ."

"You can depend on The Fonz, Dad," Richie said.

"I hope so." Howard sighed drearily. "But I'd feel a little more confident if he was building that secret bike out of something a bit practical than a bed sheet and a water pipe."

The next day, Howard drove Richie and Potsie and Ralph to the lake with a load of lumber so they could begin building the takeoff ramp that Fonzie would use to get him started on his jump across the wide end of the lake. When they arrived there, they saw Friendly Foster directing a crew of workmen at the other end.

"He's setting up for his trick riding contest," Howard said bitterly. "I ought to go down there and mix in some mortar with that sand and then pray for a tidal wave."

"What for?" Ralph asked.

Richie explained. "Mortar and sand and water make cement," he said. "The bikers wouldn't want to do any trick riding on cement." He turned back to his father. "I don't think there's even been a tidal wave in a lake," he said.

"I know. That's why I mentioned praying. It would take a miracle."

Richie, Ralph, and Potsie began unloading the lumber.

"I'm going up to the bathhouse," Howard said. "There's a phone both up there. I'm going to make a call and find out how business is."

"Dad, we only left the Biketeria about an hour ago," Richie said. "Not much could have happened since then."

"I'm not going to call the Biketeria. I'm going to call Friendly Foster's. I want to know if that price cut is doing him as much good as it could be doing us if he hadn't stolen it from us, the thief!" He set out across the sand. "Now is the time to call," he said. "Friendly Foster isn't there. Maybe his spy will answer the phone and I'll recognize his voice."

As he continued across the beach, Howard saw Friendly Foster leave the workmen and head toward the bathhouse too. Howard began running. Friendly Foster, spotting him, also began running. They reached the telephone booth at the same time, panting. As they both tried to get into the booth first, they became stuck in the opening, back to back.

"This is my booh!" Howard shouted.

"It's a public booth! I was here first!"

"I thought of using the phone first!" Howard shouted.

"I thought of it first!" Friendly Foster insisted. "I thought of it when I first woke up this morning!"

"So did I! What time did you wake up?"

"Oh, no you don't! What time did *you* wake up?"

"I didn't wake up!" Howard countered. "I didn't sleep last night. I stayed up thinking about this call I was going to make this morning!"

"Move!" Friendly Foster raged. "My call takes priority! It's a business call. I'm going to call my store!"

"I'm going to call your store, too!" Howard shouted.

"Hah! Spy!"

"That's gall—calling me a spy!" Howard said. "Your spy is a saboteur!"

"How would you like to be wearing your teeth around your neck on a string!"

"You're an insult thief, too!" Howard charged. "You stole that from me!"

"Who're you calling a thief!"

"If the shoe fits, put it on!"

"You're the insult thief!" Friendly Foster fumed. "I told you if the shoe fits put it on first!"

Howard rested, gasping for breath.

"Oh, man, this is hard work, this war," Friendly Foster said exhausted. "I haven't been this pooped since I ran the hundred-yard dash in high school."

"Were you . . . were you a dash man . . . ?" Howard said. "I went out for the mile . . ."

"No kidding?" Friendly Foster said. "What did you do it in?"

"An hour-and-a-half," Howard replied. "I only went out for the mile, I didn't make it."

Friendly Foster laughed. "I only ran about twenty-five yards of the hundred-yard dash," he confessed.

They panted quietly for a few moments, not speaking.

"This is kind of silly, this war," Friendly Foster said finally.

"It's stupid," Howard said. "I shouldn't even be in the used bike business. My hardware store is more than enough work for me."

"No, it's not your fault," Friendly Foster said. "You're entitled to be in any business you want. I just got a little scared, I guess, when I saw a competitor moving in on my territory."

"We probably ought to call the war off," Howard said.

"Yeah. Except that I've already committed myself to this trick riding contest."

"My trick riding contest," Howard said. "It was my idea first."

"Look, buddy, you are not the first one to ever think of a trick riding contest."

"No," Howard replied grimly, "and I don't suppose you're the first one to ever steal a trick riding contest, either."

"Don't start that again!" Friendly Foster warned.

"Start? You're the one who declared war!"

"You're the one who moved in on my territory!" Friendly Foster raged. "Why didn't you stay in your own backyard, fatty!"

"Fatty! Don't call me fatty, you ape!"

"Watch it, bubblehead!"

"Rat!"

"Heel!"

"Swine!"

"Stinker!"

"Snake!"

"Polecat!"
"Louse!"
"Pipsqueak!"
"Rat!"
"You already used that."
"Sorry. Fink!"
"Skunk!"

SEVEN

On the day of the proposed leap across the wide end of the lake and the trick riding contest, Howard was the first one in the Cunningham house to rise. He was up at dawn. And a short while later, Fonzie was awakened by the sound of someone climbing the ladder that Magda had placed against the house under his window a few days earlier. Curious—and somewhat groggy—Fonzie got up and went to the window, arriving just in time to see Howard appear.

"This is the first time I ever heard of a Peeping Howard," Fonzie said. "When did you take over for Tom?"

"I'm not peeping!" Howard replied. "I was on my way to the roof to— To— To—"

"You don't have to explain to me," Fonzie said. "I'm just glad that you're not up here on account of you think that ladder is the detour to the basement."

"All right, I confess!" Howard said. "I was trying to get a peek at your secret bike. Everything depends on it. Is it ready?"

"It's ready," Fonzie replied. "Get everybody up and

come around to the door and I'll let you in—that is, unless the whole family wants to surprise me and drop in on me on the way up the ladder to the roof."

"I'll wake them!" Howard said excitedly, beginning a hurried descent.

Back inside the house, Howard woke Marion, then Richie, then Joanie. They gathered outside the door to Fonzie's room.

"We're here!" Howard called in.

"I heard you," Fonzie replied, opening the door. "You sounded like a herd of mice in hikers' boots." He stepped back. "There she is!" he said, gesturing.

The Cunninghams crowded into the room. What they found was a vehicle that looked like the fallout after an explosion in a motorcycle factory. In the middle was a motorcycle sidecar, with a pair of handlebars. The sidecar was mounted on four wheels. At the sides were what appeared to be narrow lateral doors. Behind the seat in the sidecar was what looked like a metal breadbox. The engine was attached to the rear, like an outboard motor for a boat.

"That?" Howard said, stunned and dismayed. "That is what you're going to jump the wide end of the lake on?"

"Not on, in," Fonzie replied. "I sit there in the seat."

"Isn't that the breadbox I threw out a few years ago?" Marion asked.

"You didn't throw it far enough," Fonzie replied. "I found it down the basement when I went looking for a piece of pipe."

"Where is the piece of pipe?" Richie asked, looking closely at the secret bike. "I don't see it on here."

"It's not on there. I was using the piece of pipe to do the pounding, after I broke the hammer."

"The sheet," Marion said. "I don't see the sheet."

"There is more to this bike than meets the eye,'" Fonzie replied.

Howard was finally recovering from the initial shock. "Fonzie, this is a joke, isn't it?" he said hopefully. He began looking around the room. "You're hiding the real secret bike somewhere else, aren't you?"

"You might as well pull your eyeballs back in," Fonzie answered. "This, what you're looking at, is it, the real and one and only secret bike."

Howard groaned. His whole body sagged.

"Don't worry, dear," Marion said. "That was always my lucky breadbox. That might help."

"Heyyyy—ye of little faith!" Fonzie said. "What's to worry about? When The Fonz says this secret bike will jump the wide end of the lake, it will jump the wide end of the lake."

"I don't know, Fonz . . ." Richie said, looking doubtful. "Are you sure you remember how wide the wide end of the lake is? I can see this secret bike jumping that puddle we always get in front of the garage doors when it rains—maybe—but the wide end of the lake . . ." He shook his head.

"That's because what you're looking at is the bike part," Fonzie said. "What you *can't* see is the secret part."

"Where is the secret part?" Howard asked, looking around the room again. "In the closet? Under the bed?"

"When the time comes, the secret part will reveal itself," Fonzie promised. "Until then, I am not taking any chances with spies and sabotagers." He motioned to Richie. "Let's get this secret bike out of here and out to the lake," he said. "You push from the front and I'll push from behind."

As the others watched, Richie and Fonzie rolled the secret bike to the doorway—then halted.

"It's too wide, Fonz," Richie said.

Fonzie corrected him. "It's too narrow," he said.

"I'm talking about the secret bike. It's too wide for the doorway."

"The doorway was built first," Fonzie argued. "And when they built it, they built it too narrow. That is *dumb!*"

"What do we do now, bring the wide end of the lake up here to your room?" Howard asked, disgusted.

"Not through my living room!" Marion protested.

"Let me think," Fonzie said.

"We'll just have to tear out the wall," Richie said.

"Why don't you—" Joanie began.

"Heyyy—here's what I'll do," Fonzie said, interrupting. "I'll rev up the motor and get a good steam up, then I'll blast through the doorway!"

"Why don't you—" Joanie began again.

"Or maybe you could jump the secret bike out the window," Richie said.

"The bike is wider than the window, too," Howard pointed out.

"Dad, let's face it," Richie said, "there is no way to get this bike out of here without doing some damage to the house."

"Why don't you take the bike apart, then carry the parts outside and put the bike together again?" Joanie said.

There was silence.

"I guess we *can* do it that way," Fonzie said finally. "But it sure take's a lot of the fun out of it."

"Do it that way," Howard said. "Replacing the walls would take a lot of the fun out of it, too."

"I guess I don't have to take the whole thing apart," Fonzie said. "Just the wheels will probably be enough. You go out to the lake and keep an eye on that ramp, so no sabotagers get at it," he said to Howard, "and Richie can stay here and help me with the secret bike, and, sooner or later, we'll be along."

"Don't be late!" Howard said. "Don't disappoint the spectators. They're all potential customers."

"Before the day is over, I'm afraid I *got* to disappoint them," Fonzie replied.

"Because they are going to be out there at that lake expecting me to take a dive in the drink," Fonzie replied. "And I am not going to do it. I am going to jump that wide end of the lake—as advertised."

Howard looked at the secret bike. "Just to be on the safe side, I'm going to be doing a lot of praying," he said.

When Howard, Marion and Joanie arrived at the lake, a huge crowd had already gathered around the ramp. They were met by Potsie and Ralph.

"This is the biggest thing since World War II!" Ralph said excitedly. "Nobody is down at the narrow end of the lake at the trick riding contest—except the trick riders! Everybody is here!"

"Everybody except Friendly Foster, I suppose," Howard said happily.

"No, he's here," Potsie said. "I saw him in the crowd a few minutes ago. His contest hasn't started yet."

"Where's Fonzie?" Ralph asked. "Where's Richie? Where's the secret bike?"

Howard explained the delay.

"You better tell this crowd what's going on," Potsie said. "They're expecting Fonzie to show up any minute."

"Yeah, things could get ugly," Ralph said. "They're out here expecting to see Fonzie take a dive into the drink—at the very least. And if—"

"What do you mean 'at the very least?'" Marion asked.

"Well ... the local undertaker is here," Ralph replied. "And he came in his hearse."

"Oh, Howard!" Marion said. "Is it really that dangerous?"

"Marion, Fonzie knows what he's doing."

"But the wide end of the lake is so wide! And Fonzie's secret bike is so— So— So—"

"I agree with you, there are no words to describe it," Howard said. "But Fonzie obviously has confidence in it." He looked about at the faces of the spectators. "Ralph is right, though ... I better talk to this crowd," he said. "It could get ugly if they think Fonzie has backed out. That would be bad for business."

"I'd think you'd be more concerned about Fonzie," Marion said.

"I am concerned about Fonzie. The Biketeria is *his* business, too."

Howard set out through the crowd, making his way toward the ramp. At the same time, Friendly Foster appeared a short distance away from where Marion and Joanie and Potsie and Ralph were standing.

"He has sneaky eyes," Marion said.

"Are you just noticing that now, after all the years you've been married to him?" Ralph said.

"Not Howard. I'm talking about Friendly Foster. Howard has lovely eyes. Although . . . I've noticed lately that they have a tendency to look a little like dollar signs . . ."

Howard mounted the ramp. "Friends of the Biketeria!" he called out, addressing the crowd. "I have an announcement—"

"Get on with the death-defying!" a spectator shouted.

"If you'll just bear with us . . ." Howard continued. "There has been a slight hitch in our plans—"

"Booo!" Friendly Foster shouted.

Howard continued. "The Fonz will be here . . . uh . . . soon . . ."

"Fraud!" Friendly Foster bellowed. "The Fonz is yellow! It's a fake! Booooo! Fraud!"

A few of the other spectators began to boo.

"Please . . . please . . ." Howard pleaded. "The Fonz will be here . . . eventually. . . . In the meantime, we have all this sand here that isn't being used. Why don't we have a little castle-building contest? I know that some of my happiest hours—"

"Fraud!" Friendly Foster shouted again.

"Get on with the terrible family tragedy!" another spectator shouted.

"That's the undertaker," Potsie explained to Marion.

"If you'll just be patient—" Howard begged.

"Let's all go to Friendly Foster's trick riding contest down at the narrow end of the lake!" Friendly Foster called out. "We know we won't be cheated there! What Friendly Foster promises, Friendly Foster delivers!"

"No, wait—!" Howard said.

But the crowd was already on the move, trudging through the sand toward the narrow end of the lake, led by Friendly Foster. When the spectators had all gone, Marion, Joanie, Potsie, and Ralph joined Howard at the ramp.

"Don't worry, dear," Marion said. "They'll all come back as soon as Fonzie arrives."

"I don't know, Marion. . . . I'm not sure . . ."

"Believe me, dear, they'll be back," she said. "They have their hearts set on a terrible family tragedy."

"She's right, Mr. Cunningham," Potsie said. "The undertaker spoke for all of them."

"Well . . . maybe . . ." Howard looked toward the road. "Where are they? Where is Fonzie? Where is Richie? Where is the secret bike?"

"Maybe Fonzie couldn't get it back together after he took it apart," Joanie said.

"We should have ripped out that wall," Howard said.

"That wouldn't have helped, really," Marion said. "The front door would have been too narrow for the secret bike to pass through, too."

"We should have torn the house down," Howard said.

"Would I be a traitor if I went down and watched the trick riding contest?" Ralph asked.

"No . . . all of us might as well go down and watch it," Howard said. "Maybe it'll get our minds off our coming bankruptcy."

"I wasn't thinking about bankruptcy, dear," Marion said.

"She's the traitor," Howard told Ralph.

When they reached the narrow end of the lake a short while later, Friendly Foster was addressing the spectators.

"As you can see," Foster was saying, "this is not just a trick riding contest! It's also an obstacle race! And that's almost an iron-clad guarantee that there will be a lot of wrecks!"

The crowd cheered.

"The riders will do their tricks," Friendly Foster went on, "as they circle the track, meeting obstacle after obstacle. On the first turn, we have a water hole—six feet deep. To qualify for this contest, all riders have had to pass the Red Cross swimming test!"

The crowd booed.

"It's not as bad as it sounds," Friendly Foster assured the spectators. "Red Cross swimmers or not, someone could get cramps. And there are no life preservers in that six-foot deep water hole!"

The crowd cheered.

"This could turn out very well for us," Howard said to Marion, Joanie, Potsie, and Ralph, as Friendly Foster continued describing the obstacles. "If we can beat Friendly Foster to the wrecks and buy up the bikes, we can turn his contest to our advantage!"

"Howard, is that fair?"

"He stole the contest from us in the first place, didn't he? Was *that* fair?"

"Still, two unfairs don't make a fair, Howard."

"Why do I have to keep reminding everybody that fairness has nothing to do with this? This is business!"

They turned their attention back to Friendly Foster, who was concluding his explanation of the trick riding contest obstacle race.

"And just before the Finish Line," Foster was saying. "the riders come to this elastic net. Some of them, when they hit it, will probably be catapulted back to the Starting Line. Others will undoubtedly be hurled off in other directions—and where they'll land—and in what condition—we can only guess."

From the crowd came wild cheering and whistling.

"That Foster is a fiend!" Howard said. "He doesn't care what happens to those bikers! We've got to do something to help them!"

"What can we do, Dad?" Joanie asked.

"What I just suggested a couple minutes ago—we can beat Foster to those wrecked bikes. That will be Foster's punishment."

"But how will it help the bikers, Howard?" Marion asked.

"It will be their revenge," he told her. "They'll be beholden to us. Mention that to them when you bid on their bikes and maybe out of gratitude they'll sell cheap."

"When *we* bid on their bikes, Mr. Cunningham?" Potsie asked.

The bikers were now lining up at the starting line, gunning their engines.

"We've got to run this like a military operation," Howard told Potsie and Marion and Joanie and Ralph. "I'll stay here at the command post, spotting wrecks, then send you, my scouts, out to do the buying. Foster, alone, can only get to one wrecked biker at a time. But, with all of us working together, we can get to four at a time. We'll out-buy him four-to-one."

"Howard, I absolutely—" Marion began.

At that moment, the starting gun was fired. Marion's words were drowned out by the combined roar of the crowd and roar of the motorcycles.

"Howard—" Marion began again.

"Private Potsie!" Howard shouted, pointing.

A biker and his bike had plunged into the water hole. Potsie set out running to try to buy the bike.

"There goes Friendly Foster!" Joanie said. "He's after that bike, too!

"Pay any price!" Howard shouted after Potsie. "The sky's the limit!"

Another biker and his bike dropped into the water hole, sinking out of sight.

"Here's where our strategy pays off!" Howard said. "Private Ralph—Go!"

Ralph raced toward the water hole.

"While Foster is busy bidding against Potsie, Ralph will have that second biker all to himself!" Howard said.

The biker who was leading in the race was now doing one of his tricks, standing on his head on the seat, as he approached the second obstacle, a row of barrels that would have to be jumped.

"He'll never make it!" Howard said. "Private Joanie—Go!"

Joanie set off across the sand.

At the same moment, Potsie returned, soaking wet. "I had to rescue the biker first, sir," he reported to Howard, "but I bought the bike!"

"Good work, Private!" Howard pointed again. "Another biker in the water hole! Private Marion—Go!"

"General Howard—sit on it!" Marion replied.

He stared at her, stunned. "Private, you've just refused to obey a direct order! Do you realize what that is?"

"I certainly do," Marion replied. "It's good sense. If I got the wet sandy mud in that water hole splashed on this dress, I'd never get the stains out!"

"I'll go, sir!" Potsie said. "I'm not wearing my best dress."

"Go!"

As Potsie raced off, Ralph returned.

"Mission accomplished, sir," Ralph reported. "I bought the bike!"

"Two more bikes down at the barrel jump!" Howard said. "Go again!"

Ralph departed once more.

"Two bikes, Marion," Howard said. "You're supposed to go, too."

"I've thought it over and I've decided to let you court-martial me instead," Marion told him.

"Marion, I'm not doing this for me, I'm doing it for the business! Don't you care what happens to the business?"

"Right now, Howard, I know what I hope happens to the business," she replied. "I hope it drowns in the water hole!"

"Marion!"

"This business has turned you into a monster!" she charged.

"But, Marion—"

Friendly Foster came rushing up, red-faced. "You're stealing the trick riding contest I stole from you!" he charged. "I'm suing!"

"On what grounds?" Howard asked smugly.

"Underhanded over-bidding!"

"It's a free country! I can bid as high as I want to!"

Joanie returned. "I got the bike, Dad!"

Howard pointed. "A bike just bounced off the elastic net!"

Joanie raced off.

Friendly Foster ran after her. "No bidding by minors allowed!" he shouted.

Potsie and Ralph returned.

"Altogether, three more bikes, sir!" Potsie reported.

"We're cornering the market, sir," Ralph said. "And that's not easy to do on a round racetrack."

"There'll be medals for everybody when this is over," Howard said. He glanced at Marion. "For everybody but the slackers."

"Is she getting the firing squad, sir?" Ralph asked.

"If you shoot me," Marion threatened, "you can just find someone else to do the cooking and cleaning at home!"

"She's bluffing, sir!" Ralph told Howard. "Order the execution!"

"Let's not get carried away," Howard said. "I don't see how—"

At that moment, a spectator cried out. "It's The Fonz!"

Howard, Marion, Potsie, and Ralph looked toward the wide end of the lake. Fonzie and Richie had arrived at the ramp with the secret bike.

"On to the terrible family tragedy!" the undertaker shouted.

The crowd stampeded, heading for the wide end the lake. The trick riders, deserting the contest, set out in that direction too.

"It's going to be over before we get there," Potsie

said, as he and Howard and Marion and Ralph trailed after the bikers and the spectators.

"No, Fonzie wouldn't jump without me," Howard said. "I'm his partner."

"Are you going to jump with him, Howard?" Marion asked.

"There are partners and there are partners," he replied. "Fonzie is the jumping partner. I'm the watching partner."

When they caught up with the crowd, Fonzie and Richie, with the assistance of two spectators, were lifting the secret bike up onto the ramp.

"What took you so long?" Howard asked.

"Stupidity," Richie replied. "When we got the bike out of Fonzie's room, Fonzie put it together again, then we took it downstairs. But when we got to the front door, the front door wasn't wide enough either. So, Fonzie had to take it apart again before we could get it out of the house. That was the problem—it was that stupid front door."

With the bike on the ramp, Fonzie shaded his eyes and looked off across the wide end of the lake. "Has somebody been fooling around with this lake?" he asked. "It looks wider than I remember it."

Friendly Foster, standing near by, immediately began shouting to the crowd. "He's backing out! Fraud!"

The spectators began booing.

Fonzie spoke to them. "Heyyyyyy! The Fonz does not back out! When the Fonz says he's gonna jump the wide end of the lake, he jumps!"

The crowd cheered.

"Arthur—goodbye . . ." Marion said, her eyes moistening.

"Hey! You sound like you're never gonna see me again."

Marion looked off across the lake. "Well ... it *is* awfully, awfully wide." She raised her eyes to the sky. "And you *are* going to be awfully, awfully high." She lowered her eyes to the water. "And it *will* be an awfully, awfully long drop."

"Marion," Howard said uncomfortably, "let's not say anything that will make Fonzie change his mind."

"Who's changing anybody's mind?" Fonzie said.

"Let's not say anything that might avert a terrible family tragedy," Marion said. "After all, certain d-e-a-t-h has nothing to do with this. This is business."

"Who's d-e-a-t-h?" Fonzie asked.

Howard looked off nervously across the lake.

"Wide," Marion said.

Howard raised his eyes to the sky.

"High," Marion said.

Howard lowered his eyes to the water.

"Splash!" Marion said.

Howard shuddered. "Fonzie, I've changed my mind," he said. "You can't do it!"

"Hey! That's what this crowd is here for! To see me do it!"

"They're not here to see you do it," Howard said, "they're here to see you *not* do it! They think you're going to fail!"

"The Fonz? Fail?" Fonzie replied incredulously.

"It's all been a mistake!" Howard said. "This war between the Biketeria and Friendly Foster, it's a terrible, terrible mistake! I can't let you pay for it!" He looked at the secret bike. "I wouldn't even send Friendly Foster up in a crate like that."

"Dad is right, Fonz," Richie said. "The business just isn't that important."

"The business?" Fonzie responded. "You think I'm doing this for the business? I'm doing this for me."

"Becoming the used bike king isn't that important, either," Richie said.

"Who wants to become the used bike king? When I said I'm doing it for me, I meant me The Fonz." He turned his eyes toward the lake. "It's something The Fonz has got to do," he said. "I know the lake is wide. I know the sky is high. I know the drop is long. But, The Fonz is The Fonz." He faced them again. "Like I say, it's something I got to do."

"But why?" Marion asked.

Fonzie looked at the lake again. "Because ... it's wet ..." he replied.

"I didn't understand the rest," Ralph said. "But that makes sense."

Fonzie began climbing up onto the ramp.

"Marion ... I'm sorry ..." Howard said. "This is my fault."

"You did your best, dear. You tried to stop him."

As Fonzie seated himself on the secret bike, the crowd became quiet.

"Excuse me," the undertaker said to Howard, "I know this is a sad time for everyone, but, still, we must be practical. Have arrangements been made for retrieving the body from the lake?"

"There isn't going to be any body," Howard replied testily. "If Fonzie says he can jump the wide end of the lake, he can do it."

"Yes, yes, I know," the undertaker said. "I just want it understood, I don't accept drippy bodies. It will have to be dried off before I take it away in my hearse. I don't want to ruin the upholstering."

Howard glared at him.

"I thought you'd understand—business is business," the undertaker said, disappointed. "But I see you're just a sentimentalist like the rest."

Fonzie switched on the motor of the secret bike.

In unison, the spectators gasped.

Fonzie revved up the engine.

"Arthur, I've changed my mind!" Marion called out. "I want my sheet back!"

"He can't hear you, Marion," Howard said. "And you can't stop him!"

"It's too late, Mom," Richie said. "He's The Fonz. He'd jump without the sheet if he had to."

"What sheet?" Potsie asked. "I don't see any sheet."

"That's right—I don't see it, either," Marion said. She began waving her arms frantically. "Arthur—you forgot your sheet!"

Fonzie, looking down, pointed to an ear.

"Oh ... it's all right," Marion said. "He has the sheet in his ear."

"No, Mom, he's telling you he can't hear you," Richie said.

Fonzie faced forward. The secret bike began moving.

The crowd cheered.

The secret bike picked up speed. The roar of the engine was ear-splitting. The secret bike zoomed upward along the ramp, then reached the end and went shooting higher and higher into the sky.

"He's going to do it!" Howard shouted.

"Perhaps I can find some towels in the bathhouse to protect the upholstering," the undertaker mused.

The secret bike was over the middle of the wide end of the lake. It suddenly lost momentum and nosed downward.

The crowd cheered.

"Poor Arthur!" Marion cried.

All at once, the doors on the sides of the secret bike flew open and wings popped out.

"My old ironing board!" Marion said, astounded.

The secret bike, caught in an updraft from the lake, soared upward.

The crowd booed.

"He's flying!" Potsie shouted.

"Fraud!" Friendly Foster bellowed. "Flying is not jumping!"

The secret bike was nearing the far side of the wide end of the lake. Again, its nose turned downward.

"He's lost the updraft!" Richie said.

"Poor Arthur!" Marion cried.

The secret bike had reached the other side, but it was hurtling downward.

"Time to warm up the motor on the old hearse," the undertaker said, starting to leave.

Suddenly, the breadbox behind Fonzie's seat flew open and a parachute popped out.

"My sheet!" Marion said, as the chute opened.

The undertaker paused, looking betrayed.

Slowly, carried by the parachute, the secret bike drifted downward, then landed gently on the other side of the wide end of the lake.

The crowd booed angrily.

In spite of the ill feeling that Fonzie's successful landing had created among the potential customers,

Howard was delighted. "Hah!" he said triumphantly to the undertaker.

The undertaker shrugged philosophically. "In my business, we have to look on the bright side," he said. "At least, my upholstery is safe."

EIGHT

When Fonzie and the Cunninghams arrived home from the lake after Fonzie's successful jump over the wide end, they found themselves faced once more with the problem of how to handle the secret bike.

"What problem?" Joanie said. "I worked it out for you before—remember?"

"Yes, just do what you did last time, only backwards," Marion said. "Take the secret bike apart, carry it into the house, put it back together, carry it upstairs, take it apart again, carry it into Fonzie's room, then reassemble it. It's so simple."

"How about this—" Richie began.

"Hold it! I am not going to make a whole life career out of taking this bike apart and putting it together again," Fonzie said. "The secret bike stays outside." He led the way into the house. "The only thing it's good for anyway," he said, "is jumping the wide end of the lake. And I got no plans for ever doing that again."

"I guess it *has* outlived its usefulness," Howard said, when they were inside.

"I think it ought to be put on display at the

Biketeria," Marion said. "After all, Mr. Lindbergh's airplane is on display at the Smithsonian Institute."

Howard looked at her perplexedly. "Is there some connection?" he asked.

"Arthur was the first one to solo across the wide end of the lake."

"Hey! What's the matter with that Smith place for the secret bike?" Fonzie asked. "If it's good enough for Lucky Lindy, The Fonz is not gonna turn down his nose at it."

"That's nose up and thumbs down," Richie said.

"Whatever."

"Well ... you can offer it to the Smithsonian if you want to," Howard said. "Whether they'll accept it or not, I don't know. The one thing I do know is that we won't be putting it on display at the Biketeria. The Biketeria is going out of business."

"Howard, you were out in the sun too long," Marion said.

He shook his head. "I've seen the light—but it wasn't the sun," he said. "When we were out at the lake and Fonzie was getting ready to jump—and risk his life—I suddenly realized what I'd become. You had the right word for it, Marion. 'A monster,' you told me."

"But a *nice* monster," Marion assured him. "You couldn't ever be a bad monster, Howard—not with your lovely smile."

"A monster, nevertheless," Howard insisted. "The only thing that interested me was becoming the used bike king of the country. I didn't care how I did it. So," he said, "I'm putting an end to it. I'm eating crow. I'm finished with that dog-eat-dog business. It's a dead duck."

"Hey! Dog-eat-dog. Eating crow. Dead duck. You want me to lose my dinner again—before I even have it?" Fonzie said.

"Dad, there's one little problem," Richie said. "The Biketeria is only half yours. You have a partner."

"That's right ... I forgot about that ..." Howard said, looking chagrined.

"Count me in," Fonzie said. "And when I say 'count me in,' I mean count me out, along with you. The business was okay while all it was was rebuilding bikes. But when that war came along, it went sour. The Fonz is not a killer, The Fonz is a lover."

"All right, partner," Howard said, "I propose that we make it official. As senior partner, I move that the Biketeria close its doors."

"I first that," Fonzie responded.

"You second it, Fonz," Richie said.

"The Fonz? Second? The Fonz is not second to no-body."

Richie nodded. "I see what you mean—you first it."

"It has been moved and firsted," Howard said, "that the Biketeria go out of business. How do we vote?"

"Howard—is it that easy?" Marion asked. "You bought a lot of wrecked bikes at the trick riding contest today. What do you plan to do with them?"

"And you have those other wrecked bikes at the shop, and the bikes that have been rebuilt but haven't been sold yet," Richie pointed out.

"I got the feeling," Fonzie said, "that no matter how I vote, I'm gonna be back in business whether I want it or not."

"No, I still want to go out of the used bike business," Howard said. "I guess I'll just have to take the loss."

"Can we afford it?" Marion asked.

"No," Howard replied. "But if I stick with used bikes, I know what will happen—I'll begin wanting to be king again. But I'll become the same old monster, instead."

"I think I got an idea," Fonzie said. "Let's close up the business and close up the house and move out of town. We can all move to Mozambique."

"I wonder if they need a king there?" Marion said.

There was a knock at the door.

Fonzie answered it and found Magda there. "I was just talking about you," he said.

She smiled sultrily. "Saying what?"

"Mozambique," he replied.

"I'm sorry I wasn't at the lake," Magda said, entering the house. "But I thought it would be a waste of time. It didn't occur to me that you could *really* jump the wide end. I thought you would end up— Well, let me put it this way: I hate good-byes."

"Yeah, I noticed that you weren't there," Fonzie replied. "I didn't know the reason, though. I thought maybe you were out looking for a ladder to climb."

"I'm so happy that everything turned out so well for you," Magda said to Howard and Fonzie. "You have more wrecked bikes to rebuild. And now, after the leap across the wide end of the lake, everyone knows about the Biketeria. I'm sure business will soon be booming."

"Actually—Howard began.

"Yeah, she's right, business will be booming," Fonzie said, interrupting.

"And the war will go on," Magda said.

"As a matter of fact—" Howard said.

Fonnzie broke in again. "She's right," he said, "it's back to the trenches."

"What will your strategy be now?" Magda asked. "I'm sure you have some new way to beat that terrible Friendly Foster."

"Oh, yeah, we got big battle plans," Fonzie said.

"We have?" Howard said, bewildered. "I thought—"

"Yeah, he's right, he thought them up," Fonzie said to Magda. "With these new battle plans, when we get finished with Friendly Foster, he's gonna change his name to Pearl Harbor—that's what his business is gonna look like."

"Oh, that sounds exciting," Magda said calmly. "What are the plans?"

"Yeah . . . what are the plans?" Fonzie replied vaguely. "Well, they're like the secret bike, they're secret."

"But you'll tell me," Magda said. "After all, I'm on your side."

"Well, first—" Fonzie began.

The phone rang.

"That's probably the cannon salesman," Fonzie said, picking up the receiver. "You can't hold a war without a cannon." He spoke into the phone. "Yeah?" he said. "No, this is not—" His expression suddenly changed. "Oh, The Fonz, you mean—The Fonz that invented the secret bike. Yeah, this is him. He listened for a moment, then spoke again. "A million? What would I do with a million dollars? I'd look like a nerd with all that cash stuffed in my pockets. I like to keep a slim silhouette."

"Did I hear what I thought I just heard?" Howard said to Marion, as Fonzie continued the telephone conversation. "Did he say a million dollars?"

"That's what he said," Marion replied. "Our phone must be out of order."

"Out of order?"

"That's the only explanation I can think of. It's never said a million dollars before. Its wires must be crossed."

"That makes a difference," Fonzie said into the receiver. "I thought all you wanted was the secret bike. But if you want the Biketeria, too, that's a horse of a different color—a lot greener. Maybe two million bucks."

"You're right, Marion, the phone is out of order," Howard said. "I thought I just heard Fonzie ask for two million dollars for the Biketeria and the secret bike. Why would anybody be willing to pay—"

"I got to think about it," Fonzie said into the phone. "I got a partner to talk it over with. Give me another call in a couple days." He hung up.

"What? What? What?" Howard said anxiously.

"Dumb," Fonzie replied.

"Dumb?"

"That's the only word for it," Fonzie said. "What would you say if some big bike company called you up on the phone and wanted to buy the secret bike? Dumb."

"Don't blame the bike company, Arthur," Marion said. "It's the phone—it's out of order."

"Dumb? What's so dumb about it?" Howard asked Fonzie. "Why do they want it?"

"What would you say if I told you they wanted to sell it to old middle-aged codgers?"

Howard drew himself up. "I wouldn't care much for the 'codgers' crack," he replied. "What are you telling me? That a big bike company wants to manufacture the secret bike? And sell it to the middle-age market?"

"What would you say if I told you they wanted to put two more wheels on it?" Fonzie said.

"It already has four wheels," Richie said. "They want to make it a six-wheeler?"

"What would you say if I told you that, with six wheels and wings and a parachute, they figure it would be safe enough for old middle-aged codgers to ride?"

"It makes sense to me," Howard said. "Did they actually offer you a million dollars?"

"That's just a figure to talk about," Fonzie replied. "A bike company that would be so dumb would probably tell the guy that invented the secret bike that he'd get a cut on every bike they could sell. They might talk about a figure like a million dollars—but, who knows?"

"What was that about the Biketeria?" Richie asked. "Why do they want the shop, too?"

"What would you say if I told you this bike company said they had to have stores to sell the secret bike to old middle-aged codgers from, so they figured they'd start with the Biketeria?"

"Why do you keep asking us what we'd say?" Joanie asked.

"I like to get everybody's opinion. I wonder what Friendly Foster, for instance, would say?"

"What's he got to do with it?" Howard asked.

"Well, you know what would happen if some big bike company came in here and ran the Biketeria," Fonzie said. "They wouldn't want no competition from some little guy like Friendly Foster. They'd cut their prices and run him out of business. It wouldn't bother them to lose a little money for a while."

"Excuse me," Magda said, heading for the door. "I just remembered—I have to wash my hair." The door closed behind her.

"That was awfully sudden," Marion said, puzzled. "Her hair looked fine to me."

"Maybe that wasn't her real reason," Fonzie suggested. He went to the door and opened it. "I think we will be having some unexpected company in a couple minutes," he said, returning and leaving the door ajar.

"Somebody from the bike company?" Howard asked. "Are they sending someone to make us an offer?"

"What bike company is that?" Fonzie asked innocently.

"The dumb bike company, dear," Marion said.

"I don't see anything dumb about it," Howard said. "As a matter of fact, now that I've had a chance to think about it, I'm not so sure that we should sell out. As I said before, the market is wide open for a bike for middle-agers. If we could work out some way to manufacture the secret bike ourselves—"

"Heyyyyyyyyy!" Fonzie said. "We already been through that. What do you want to be now, the secret bike king?"

"You'll just turn out to be the secret monster, Howard," Marion warned.

"Besides, half that million dollars is going to be yours," Joanie reminded her father. "What more do you want?"

"Compared to what that bike company will make

on the secret bike, a half-million dollars is peanuts,"
Howard argued.

"About that ... don't go counting your half-million
peanuts before they're shelled," Fonzie said. "You
only heard my side of that telephone conversation.
There could be some details that might make you
change your mind about what you want to do."

Howard looked at him warily. "What kind of details?"

"I'm no lawyer," Fonzie replied. "What would you
say if some lawyer told you that sometimes what you
think you hear over the telephone is not what somebody was saying after all?"

"Why are we starting this 'What would you say?'
business again?" Howard asked.

"Fonz, we weren't mistaken, we did hear you say 'a
million dollars' when you were talking on the phone,
didn't we?" Richie asked.

"That you did. I said it—a million dollars. Only—"

At that instant, Friendly Foster came rushing into
the house.

"Hey, surprise!" Fonzie said. "Here's that unexpected
company we been expecting."

"I'm not going to beat around the bush!" Friendly
Foster said angrily. "You can't do it! Have I made
myself clear? I'll sue! I'll fight fire with fire! I'll cut
prices down to the bone! *Past* the bone! I'll take this
to the Supreme Court! Milwaukee for Milwaukeeans!"

"We don't know what you're talking about," Fonzie
replied. "Because you couldn't possibly know what
you sound like you're talking about on account of you
weren't here when the telephone call came."

"Don't tell me I don't know what I'm talking
about!" Friendly Foster raged. "I know the whole

story. You're plotting with some big bike company to ruin me!"

"*How* do you know that?" Fonzie asked.

"I know because— Well, I know because . . . uh . . ."

"I knew there was something wrong with our phone," Marion said. "Mr. Foster has been getting our calls."

"Yes! The wires were crossed!" Friendly Foster said. "By accident, I happened to overhear your conversation with that big bike company."

"Which big bike company was it?" Fonzie asked.

"Oh . . . let's see, which big bike company was it? Well, actually, I came in on the middle of the conversation. All I heard was the plotting, the plan to ruin me, to run me out of business." He raised his right hand. "And I'll swear to that in court!"

"You would swear in court that Monday is Tuesday," Fonzie said. "Your mother named you too fast when she named you Friendly. If she'd waited a while, she would have named you 'Crooked.'"

"Slander!" Foster cried. "I'll sue you for slander, too! You heard him," he said to the others. "You're my witnesses!"

"What do you need them for?" Fonzie asked. "Your spy is all the witness you need. When she gets in court, she can tell everything that anybody said around the Biketeria—and, today, everything that everybody said here at the house."

"Spy?" Friendly Foster asked.

"And while she's at it, she can testify how—with you telling her what to do—she sabotaged those bikes at the Biketeria," Fonzie continued. "The court ought to be very interested in that. Everybody likes a good spy story."

"I don't know what spy you're talking about."

"I think I can give you a hint," Marion said. "She has dirty hair."

"Magda? I hardly know the girl. To me, she's just a stranger in town," Friendly Foster said.

"Yeah, I noticed that the first time you saw her you said, 'Hello, stranger in town,'" Foster said. "How did you know she was a stranger in town?"

"Hah—gotcha!" Friendly Foster replied. "I knew she was a stranger because I hadn't ever seen her before!"

"Are you telling me you know everybody in Milwaukee on sight?" Fonzie asked. "You're gonna have some trouble selling a story like that to the court. Maybe Milwaukee is not New York, but it is not Mozambique, either."

"I confess!" Friendly Foster said suddenly. "Yes, Magda was my spy! But, have mercy! Don't sell the Biketeria to that big bike company! They'll run me out of business!"

"That didn't bother you when you were the runner and we were the runnee," Fonzie pointed out.

"But I've changed!" Friendly Foster said. "I was a bad guy, yes, but I'm a good guy now—and us good guys have got to stick together."

"Against who?" Howard asked. "Who is the bad guy now?"

"That big bike company," Friendly replied. "What do you think they're in business for? To drive us good guys out, that's why! Don't sell the Biketeria to them," he begged, "sell it to me!"

"Maybe we could do that . . ." Fonzie said.

"No, we *can't* do that!" Howard told him. "That big

bike company is willing to pay a million dollars for the Biketeria. Foster won't pay that much!"

"You're in error on that," Foster said to Howard. "According to my spy, the big bike company is paying a million for the secret bike. They only want the Biketeria so they'll have a place to sell secret bikes when they begin manufacturing them. But I could do that for them if I owned the Biketeria. I'm not the kind of guy who holds a grudge."

"Isn't that wonderful!" Marion said, delighted. "He really is one of us good guys now!"

"Yeah," Fonzie said to Howard, "I don't think there's any big bike company that cares whether it has the Biketeria or not. So, if we're gonna sell out, we might as well sell out to some guy that's local from Milwaukee."

"Milwaukee for Milwaukeeans!" Friendly Foster cried out.

"Hold it down, will you?" Fonzie said. "You sound like a cheerleader for Adolph Hitler." He turned back to Howard. "Okay, partner, we sell out to Friendly Foster?"

"Well—"

"It's a chance to get back all that money you put into the business, Dad," Richie said. "You might even make a profit."

"Nah, we don't want to make no profit on a fellow good guy," Fonzie said. "We'll sell out to Foster for exactly the amount of money we got invested."

"Fonz, I think we could get a lot more than that," Richie said.

"No, Fonzarelli is right," Friendly Foster said. "I'll pay you exactly what you have invested—or perhaps a little less. I'm not in business for my health, you know. As a matter of fact—"

"You're gonna pay us what we got in the business," Fonzie told him, "or it's no deal."

"I'm going to pay you exactly what you have in the business," Foster said, cowed.

"That's almost two-thousand dollars, according to the books," Richie said.

"We'll make it two-thousand even," Friendly Foster said, getting out his checkbook. "Also, I'll draw up a little contract that we can all sign, and that will make it legal."

"I have a feeling that we're making a mistake," Howard said to Fonzie, as Foster began writing out the contract on a scrap of paper. He shrugged. "But, I suppose it doesn't really matter, since we're getting a million for the secret bike."

"That's quite a profit," Foster commented. "How much money do you have in that secret bike?"

"A hundred dollars," Fonzie told him.

"Uh-huh ... a hundred dollars ..." Foster mused, still writing the contract.

"Put on that piece of paper that you know what you're getting, two-thousand dollars worth of wrecked bikes and rebuilt bikes for two-thousand dollars," Fonzie said to Foster.

"Oh, sure ..."

"That *is* what you're getting, that and nothing more, you understand, don't you?" Fonzie said.

"Righto!" He handed the contract to Howard. "If you'll just sign this ..."

Howard signed.

"And you," Foster said, passing the contract along to Fonzie.

Fonzie glanced at it, then signed.

"Now, I'll put my signature to it," Friendly Foster said, writing.

"Why do I still feel that we're making a mistake?" Howard asked.

Having signed the contract, Foster handed the check to Howard. "This makes it a deal," he said. "No backing out now."

Howard looked at the check. "I'm not the one who made the mistake, you are," he said to Foster. "This check is for two-thousand dollars and an extra one-hundred dollars."

Foster grinned widely. "That's no mistake. Read the contract."

Howard read. The color began draining from his face. Enraged, he tried to protest, but only sputtered.

"Dad—what's the matter?" Richie asked.

"He owns the secret bike!" Howard exploded. "He bought it for a hundred dollars—exactly what Fonzie invested in it!"

"Gee whillikers!" Fonzie said, in mock surprise. "You mean there has been skullduggery afoot?"

"Oh, no!" Foster said. "It's all fair and square. You signed that contract. You both signed it! We all signed it! It's legal!"

"Let's face it, Mr. Cunningham," Fonzie said. "We been out-smarted. There's nothing we can do about it."

Howard began sputtering again.

"But Fonz, you can't let him get away with that," Richie said. "He's getting a million dollar bike for a hundred dollars!"

"That's what it looks like," Fonzie agreed. "That sure is what it looks like."

"Now, you can tell me the name of that big bike company," Friendly Foster said to Fonzie.

"What big bike company is that?"

"Oh, I get it—you've got no sense of humor," Friendly Foster said. "Just because you think I swindled you, you refuse to tell me the name of the company. Well, that doesn't matter. When that big bike company comes to town to buy the secret bike, they'll have to deal with me!"

"I don't remember telling you anything about a big bike company," Fonzie said. "You're the one who mentioned the big bike company, which you learned about from your spy."

Friendly Foster chuckled. "I know what your game is," he told Fonzie. "You're trying to trick me, trying to make me think that there is no big bike company that made you an offer for the secret bike. But, you forget—my spy heard the whole telephone conversation!"

"Gee whillikers again," Fonzie said.

"We'll sue!" Howard threatened.

Friendly Foster waved the contract. "Sue away! It's all in writing—signed, sealed, and delivered." Chortling, he headed for the door. "I'm off! On my million-dollar secret bike!"

The door closed behind him.

"I should have told him never to open the parachute in a stiff breeze," Fonzie said. "It makes the secret bike go faster backwards than frontwards."

Howard sank into his chair, moaning.

"Fonz, I don't understand this," Richie said. "It isn't like you to let somebody get away with something like that. Don't you realize what's happened?"

"Sure I realize what's happened," Fonzie replied.

"We're even. We put two-thousand dollars and a hundred dollars into the Biketeria and the secret bike and now we got it back."

From outside came the roar of an engine as Friendly Foster departed on the secret bike.

"A million dollars—off in a cloud of dust!" Howard groaned.

"Dad is right," Richie said to Fonzie. "*That* is what has happened, Friendly Foster got a million dollar bike for a hundred dollars!"

Fonzie shook his head. "What Foster got was a hundred-dollar bike for a hundred dollars," he said. "He got exactly what he paid for—a two-thousand-dollar business for two-thousand dollars and a hundred-buck bike for a hundred bucks. Us and Friendly Foster are all square."

"But, Fonz . . . the big bike company . . . the million-dollar offer . . ."

"What big bike company?"

"The phone call—" Howard said, sitting up.

"That was a wrong number," Fonzie told him.

"Fonz, you told us it was a big bike company calling!" Richie said.

"Did I? As I remember, what I said was, 'What would you say if a big bike company called.' I didn't say it was, all I did was ask what you would say if it was. There is a big difference in that."

There was silence for a moment as the others began to realize what had happened.

"And Magda—" Howard said.

"Yeah, I figured she was the spy and sabotager," Fonzie said. "So, I tossed a million-dollar bet out on the table just to see if she'd call. She did. She called Friendly Foster."

"How did you guess that she was a spy?" Joanie asked.

"Nobody that cool could be that dumb," Fonzie replied. "It had to be an act."

Howard was now smiling. "I know what will happen next," he said. "Friendly Foster will wait for that big bike company to contact him. When it doesn't happen, he'll start calling all the big bike companies in the country, trying to sell them a four-wheeled motorcycle with wings and a parachute for a million dollars."

"If it weren't for Fonzie, that could be you, Howard," Marion said.

"You're right," he replied. "Inside me, I'm afraid, I have a monster."

"That could explain the chubbiness," Fonzie said. "You got two of you in there."

"I've learned my lesson," Howard said. "That monster is never going to get out again. I'm going to stick to the hardware business."

"And I'm going back to my job at the garage," Fonzie said.

"I guess you won't be seeing Magda any more," Richie said to him. "That's kind of a shame. She was really cool."

"Nah, I think we broke even on that, too," Fonzie said. "She wasn't cool. She only sounded cool. There is a big difference between a put on cool and a real cool, you know. What her cool was, it was just the draft escaping from a cold heart."

The others looked at him, puzzled.

"Like when you open the refrigerator door and get a cold breeze," Fonzie said.

They continued to stare at him.

"Come on out in the kitchen," Fonzie said, leaving. "You can stand in front of the refrigerator while I open the door and get a beer. It's the only way to get to know Magda like The Fonz knows Magda."

Indian file, they trailed after him, eager to learn another little lesson in Life from The Fonz.

FILMS & TV

0352   Star

30006X	**THE MAKING OF KING KONG** B. Bahrenburg	60p*
398957	**THE MARRIAGE RING("COUPLES")** Paddy Kitchen & Dulan Barber	60p
397276	**MURDER BY DEATH** H. R. F. Keating	60p*
398825	**McCOY: THE BIG RIP-OFF** Sam Stewart	50p*
398035	**PAUL NEWMAN** Michael Kerbel	75p
397470	**ODE TO BILLY JOE** Herman Raucher	60p*
398191	**THE ROCKFORD FILES** Mike Jahn	50p*
397373	**THE SCARLET BUCCANEER** D. R. Benson	60p*
398442	**THE SIX MILLION DOLLAR MAN 3: THE** **RESCUE OF ATHENA ONE** Mike Jahn	45p*
398647	**THE SIX MILLION DOLLAR MAN 4:** **PILOT ERROR** Jay Barbree	50p*
396490	**SIX MILLION DOLLAR MAN 5:** **THE SECRET OF BIGFOOT** Mike Jahn	60p
396652	**SPACE 1999: (No. 2)** **MIND BREAKS OF SPACE** Michael Butterworth	60p
396660	**SPACE 1999 (No. 1)** **PLANETS OF PERIL** Michael Butterworth	60p
398531	**SPANISH FLY** Madelaine Duke	50p
398817	**SWITCH** Mike Jahn	50p*
398051	**THE ULTIMATE WARRIOR** Bill S. Ballinger	50p*

0426   Tandem

180240	**AT THE EARTH'S CORE** Edgar Rice Burroughs	50p
180321	**THE LAND THAT TIME FORGOT** Edgar Rice Burroughs	50p
164164	**LENNY** Valerie Kohler Smith	50p*
16184X	**ONEDIN LINE: THE HIGH SEAS** Cyril Abraham	60p
132661	**ONEDIN LINE: THE IRON SHIPS**	60p
168542	**SHAMPOO** Robert Alley	50p

*Not for sale in Canada

0352　Star

396881	A STAR IS BORN Alexander Edwards	60p
396792	THE BIONIC WOMAN (No. 1) DOUBLE IDENTITY Maud Willis	50p*
39689X	BIONIC WOMAN (No. 2) A QUESTION OF LIFE	50p*
398175	THE BLACK BIRD Alexander Edwards	45p*
398256	CANNON: THE FALLING BLONDE Paul Denver	50p*
398728	CANNON: IT'S LONELY ON THE SIDEWALK	50p*
396687	CARQUAKE Michael Avallone	60p
397349	COLUMBO: ANY OLD PORT IN A STORM Henry Clement	50p*
398183	COLUMBO: A CHRISTMAS KILLING Alfred Lawrence	45p*
300795	COLUMBO: THE DEAN'S DEATH	40p*
30099X	DIRTY HARRY Phillip Roch	60p
396903	EMMERDALE FARM (No. 1) THE LEGACY Lee Mackenzie	50p
396296	EMMERDALE FARM: (No. 2) PRODIGAL'S PROGRESS Lee Mackenzie	60p
397489	ESCAPE FROM THE DARK Rosemary Anne Sisson	50p
398744	GABLE AND LOMBARD Joe Morella & Edward Z. Epstein	60p*
397160	HARRY & WALTER GO TO NEW YORK Sam Stewart	50p*
398493	HAWAII 5-0: THE ANGRY BATTALION Herbert Harris	50p*
300876	HAWAII 5-0: SERPENTS IN PARADISE	45p*
396288	HEAVEN HAS NO FAVOURITES Erich Maria Remarque	75p
398477	HUSTLE Stephen Shagan	60p*
398574	INNOCENTS WITH DIRTY HANDS Richard Neely	60p*
397500	INSERTS Anton Rimart	60p
397438	KOJAK: GIRL IN THE RIVER Victor B. Miller	50p*
397357	KOJAK: GUN BUSINESS	50p*
397446	KOJAK: MARKED FOR MURDER	50p*
398671	KOJAK: TAKE-OVER	50p*

*Not for sale in Canada.

GENERAL FICTION

0352   Star

396423	Mary Ann Ashe **RING OF ROSES**	60p
396938	Andre P. Brink **LOOKING ON DARKNESS**	95p
398663	Jackie Collins **THE WORLD IS FULL OF DIVORCED WOMEN**	50p
398752	**THE WORLD IS FULL OF MARRIED MEN**	50p
300671	Eric Corder **HELLBOTTOM**	75p*
300086	**THE LONG TATTOO**	40p*
398515	**RUNNING DOGS**	60p*
396857	Terry Fisher **IF YOU'VE GOT THE MONEY**	70p
39840X	Knight Isaacson **THE STORE**	60p
398981	Jeffrey Konvitz **THE SENTINEL**	70p*
396334	Gavin Lambert **THE SLIDE AREA**	75p
398299	Robin Maugham **THE SIGN**	55p
397594	Clayton Moore **END OF RECKONING**	60p*
397608	**141 TERRACE DRIVE**	60p*
397543	**RIVER FALLS**	60p*
397667	**SECRET FIRE**	60p*
397659	**THE CORRUPTERS**	60p*
397551	**WESLEY SHERIDAN**	60p*
300809	Molly Parkin **LOVE ALL**	50p
397179	**UP TIGHT**	60p
396946	Judith Rossner **TO THE PRECIPICE**	85p*
397144	Alan Sillitoe **THE FLAME OF LIFE**	70p
398892	**THE GENERAL**	50p
300965	**THE LONELINESS OF THE LONG DISTANCE RUNNER**	50p
300949	**MEN, WOMEN AND CHILDREN**	50p
398809	**THE RAGMAN'S DAUGHTER**	50p
300981	**SATURDAY NIGHT AND SUNDAY MORNING**	50p
396415	Hubert Selby Jr. **THE ROOM**	75p
398884	Ernest Tidyman **STARSTRUCK**	60p*

*Not for sale in Canada.

Wyndham Books are obtainable from many booksellers and newsagents. If you have any difficulty please send purchase price plus postage on the scale below to:

Wyndham Cash Sales,
44 Hill Street
London W1X 8LB

While every effort is made to keep prices low, it is sometimes necessary to increase prices at short notice. Wyndham Books reserve the right to show new retail prices on covers which may differ from those advertised in the text or elsewhere.

Postage and Packing Rate
U.K. & Eire
One book 15p plus 7p per copy for each additional book ordered to a maximum charge of 57p.

These charges are subject to Post Office charge fluctuations.